A bullet pinged not two feet away from Ree.

Quint pulled her out of harm's way just in time to shield her from the next one. They fell into a heap on the hard Texas soil.

"We need to run," she said. "Can you?"

Quint performed a quick mental inventory of his body.

"I'll figure it out," he said. His headache alone was enough to slow him down, forget his injuries.

"Let's go," she said, linking their fingers. They ducked as low as possible to make them harder targets to hit, and took off in the opposite direction of the highway, into the blackness.

The farther away they ran from the Chevy, the thicker the underbrush became. The toe of Quint's boot got caught on it, causing him to face-plant, and Ree came down with him. Both held on to their weapons. The accidental move was where their luck would run out as shots whizzed past their heads...

MISSION HONEYMOON

USA TODAY Bestselling Author

BARB HAN

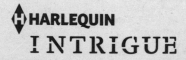

All my love to Brandon, Jacob and Tori,
the three great loves of my life.

To Babe, my hero, for being my best friend,
greatest love and my place to call home.

I love you all with everything that I am.

Recycling programs
for this product may
not exist in your area.

ISBN-13: 978-1-335-58206-5

Mission Honeymoon

Copyright © 2022 by Barb Han

All rights reserved. No part of this book may be used or reproduced in any manner whatsoever without written permission except in the case of brief quotations embodied in critical articles and reviews.

This is a work of fiction. Names, characters, places and incidents are either the product of the author's imagination or are used fictitiously. Any resemblance to actual persons, living or dead, businesses, companies, events or locales is entirely coincidental.

For questions and comments about the quality of this book, please contact us at CustomerService@Harlequin.com.

Harlequin Enterprises ULC
22 Adelaide St. West, 41st Floor
Toronto, Ontario M5H 4E3, Canada
www.Harlequin.com

Printed in U.S.A.

USA TODAY bestselling author **Barb Han** lives in north Texas with her very own hero-worthy husband, three beautiful children, a spunky golden retriever/standard poodle mix and too many books in her to-read pile. In her downtime, she plays video games and spends much of her time on or around a basketball court. She loves interacting with readers and is grateful for their support. You can reach her at barbhan.com.

Books by Barb Han

Harlequin Intrigue

A Ree and Quint Novel

Undercover Couple
Newlywed Assignment
Eyewitness Man and Wife
Mission Honeymoon

An O'Connor Family Mystery

Texas Kidnapping
Texas Target
Texas Law
Texas Baby Conspiracy
Texas Stalker
Texas Abduction

Rushing Creek Crime Spree

Cornered at Christmas
Ransom at Christmas
Ambushed at Christmas
What She Did
What She Knew
What She Saw

Decoding a Criminal

Visit the Author Profile page at Harlequin.com.

CAST OF CHARACTERS

Emmaline Ree Sheppard a.k.a. Ree—This ATF agent will do anything to protect a partner who refuses to save himself.

Quinton Casey a.k.a. Quint—This hotshot ATF agent blames himself for his pregnant partner's death and will stop at nothing to put the person responsible behind bars, placing himself in danger in the process.

Vadik Gajov—Faking his murder might be key to the investigation if he'll cooperate.

Giselle Langley—Is this mistress who she appears to be?

Lizanne Vega—This "toys and lingerie" shop owner might lead the investigation straight to Dumitru's door.

Rolph Lindberg a.k.a. Lindy—This new player seems even closer to Dumitru.

Dumitru—The ultimate target and person responsible for Tessa's murder is elusive—too much so?

Chapter One

Just breathe.

All ATF Agent Ree Sheppard felt on either side of her was a wooden box. Trapped, she wiggled her foot and felt the bottom. If she stretched out her body, the crown of her head reached the top. Her shoulders were in a permanent shrug, and she could scarcely move her arms in any direction. The space was fitted glove tight.

The sun was high in the sky on a hot mid-September afternoon. A sliver of daylight came in through a crack where the wood didn't perfectly match up. Ree lifted her head toward it, trying to grab fresh air. Panic set in as reality gripped her. She'd been hit in the back of the head after breathing in a chemical that rendered her unconscious. Or maybe it was the other way around. She couldn't be certain. She did, however, have a monster of a headache. Based on the angle of the sun, she hadn't been out for long.

And then it dawned on her what she was inside. This was a coffin. Her lungs clawed for air as her claustrophobia took the wheel. Her chest squeezed, and she had to remind herself to slow down and breathe again. This was her worst nightmare realized.

"Sit tight, sweetheart. We'll be back for you if you make it through the day and your man cooperates," the unfamiliar male voice stated with a haughty laugh. Ree had been abducted in Dallas, where she'd returned to the apartment she was sharing with her undercover partner during their last case.

"You didn't say anything about putting her in a coffin, Lindy," a female voice stated. This one was familiar. Giselle Langley was the mistress of someone mid-level in the crime organization Ree and her partner were investigating. Giselle had helped Ree and Quint climb another rung higher toward the leader before betraying Ree earlier today by luring her outside her apartment. Unbeknownst to Giselle, her imprisoned boyfriend had arranged for her to be offered Witness Protection once this case was over. Ree and Quint were on a mission to take down one of the largest and most profitable Romanian weapon trafficking rings in Texas. Giselle's link to Vadik Gajov was meant to get them one step closer to their ultimate target, Dumitru, the man in charge and responsible for the death of an agent. Tessa Kind had not only been Quint's best friend, but she'd been pregnant. The fact that she'd been able to convince Quint not to tell their boss haunted him. Locking Dumitru behind bars for the rest of his life had become Quint's sole mission. Ree's partner and, most recently, fiancé couldn't let it go. Even though Quint didn't yet have a ring, he'd asked Ree to marry him at the conclusion of their last case and she'd said yes. Still, with Dumitru walking around free, they couldn't begin their future. Not until justice was served.

"She'll be fine until we come back for her," the male voice said.

"No," Giselle argued, and there was something in her voice that sent an icy shiver racing down Ree's spine. "Don't do it, Lindy. She won't be able to breathe."

Rolph Lindberg, a.k.a. Lindy, was on the same level as Vadik according to their desk agent, Agent James Grappell. Vadik and Lindy both were advisors to Dumitru. Vadik was presently in jail due to a recent bust that Quint had orchestrated while Ree had been forced to play the part of party girl at Vadik's penthouse.

At the conclusion of their last case, Lindy had posed as Dumitru via a text message calling for Vadik's murder. Part of their cover story was that Quint had been released from prison recently and, therefore, would have connections inside. From what Ree gathered so far, she'd been abducted to force Quint into arranging for Vadik to be killed while locked up.

Lindy wasn't exactly known for mercy. Ree squirmed, testing the strength of the homemade coffin. She strained to check out what was happening aboveground in time for the first clump of dirt to hit the wood. She blinked as crumbs hit her in the eye.

"Stop." Giselle's voice was more agitated now. Nervous?

"Or what?" Lindy said. Another clump splattered

on the outside of the encasing like a pumpkin that had been thrown off a bridge.

"I'll tell Axel," she threatened. There was far less confidence in her tone now. It had raised an octave too, which wasn't exactly encouraging from where Ree stood. "They're his friends, and he wouldn't want them treated this way."

Lindy stopped. Was he considering the plea?

"I can't leave this in the open," he finally stated. "If someone finds her, it could be worse all the way around, including for her."

"Good point," she said, then hesitated.

How about someone pull me out of this grave and open the box? How about that? Ree wanted to shout.

"She's been missing for hours already," Giselle continued after a few beats. "He'll come looking for her. What if he finds her like this?"

"Are you kidding around or just stupid?" Lindy asked.

"What are you doing with your phone?" Giselle didn't come off as offended despite the dig.

"What do you think? Taking a picture," he stated like she should have read his mind. Or was it that obvious to someone in their line of work?

"Here's the deal," Giselle started. "I'm the one who asked to meet up with her for lunch. My name is on this, and on Axel's by extension. If anything happens to her, who do you think her man will come after?" She paused as though for dramatic affect. "That's right. *Me.* And when Quint puts me in a box over this, I won't ever be coming out again. And then you'll have Axel Ivan to deal with. Is that what you want?" Giselle seemed to gain more confidence the longer she spoke. "I'm not taking a hit for this one, Lindy. Now, let her out. She'll wake up any minute now. You can leave her out here in the boondocks. Who knows how long it'll take her to walk back to Dallas? By then, he will have already done what you want."

"If I open this box and she doesn't wake up right away, she might be dealing with something worse than me," Lindy said. "There's all kinds of wildlife out here. Is that what you want? You want to come back here and find her blood and guts everywhere?"

"Well, no. Not when you put it like that." She cowered.

Ree wanted to shout. She wanted to tell Giselle to go to hell for baiting her into a meetup that ended with Ree in a coffin. Instinct told her to be quiet and be still no matter how much her lungs clawed for air and she wanted to scream.

There were a couple of important points Ree picked up on in their conversation. For one, they planned on coming back, at least. Could she spend an entire day and night out here in the middle of nowhere? She listened for sounds of vehicles or a roadway and heard nothing. Another note was that even if she was able to free herself from this box, what would she do next? They'd said they were about to leave her in an area where wildlife roamed freely. A dark thought struck her. Texas was known for snakes, spiders and all manner of insects. If they left her inside this thing, who knew what could join her?

Ree shivered at the thought. She hated snakes. Spiders weren't much better in her book. But the stabbing pain in her chest would do her in before either of those had a chance at her. After growing up with four rowdy brothers on a small ranch, Ree didn't fear a whole lot of people. Being buried alive ranked right up there beside heights and small spaces, though.

More of those calming breaths, she reminded herself as she waited to hear her fate.

"See. I'm doing her a favor by covering the box," he continued.

"How will she breathe?" Giselle asked, her voice more of a whine than anything else now.

Another splat sounded. Dirt seeped through the crevice. Ree literally thought she might hyperventilate.

"Let's get out of here," Giselle said, sounding a little panicked.

Seriously? She was the one who was freaking out? Ree had a few choice words for her so-called friend when she got out of this predicament. This seemed like a good time to remind herself she was one hundred percent successful at getting herself out of difficult situations. Granted, this was the first time she'd been *buried alive*. Those last two words caused a tremor to rock her body. Biting her tongue was near impossible.

The sound of footsteps walking away from the area sent a cold chill racing up her spine. An engine came to life. It didn't sound like a truck. Could be a sedan or SUV. Did Giselle think she was going to get away with this? Did Lindy?

Clearly, they planned to leave her there—wherever *there* was—alone. A sharp pain in the back of her head reminded her of the blow she'd taken as she was being herded into a minivan. A cloth had been placed over her mouth before the rank smell filled her senses and total darkness came. The memory caused white-hot anger to roil in her veins.

Ree silently counted to sixty, marking each passing second by straightening a finger from her fists.

It was hot. There was no air movement. The box was stifling.

Beads of sweat rolled down Ree's forehead and dampened the back of her neck. There were no sounds of life. Not yet anyway. Ree needed to get out of this box and now.

Could she shimmy down a little more and kick out the bottom? There was very little wiggle room. Maybe she could blow out her breath and bring her shoulders in. She inched down. Would it be possible to take in a deep breath and cause her shoulders to swell enough to break out? The move would be faster. She tried. Failed. More of the panic tried to take hold.

She couldn't allow her nerves to take over. An anxiety attack would only make the situation worse. Logically, she knew it. Emotions were a whole different ball game.

Another attempt at trying to get her feet to the bottom made a little more progress. She grazed the wood with the ball of her foot. More wiggling and she got her heel there too. Problem. There was no room to lift her leg high enough to get off a good stomp. At this rate, she would never get out of this awful thing. Ree expanded her lungs, pushing her shoulders hard against the crate. Shock of all shocks, there was enough give to rain dirt down on her through the crevices. She turned her head and spit out the mud crumbs.

Ree turned a little on her side and threw her right elbow up. The lid loosened. A few more elbows and she was covered in soil. She sat bolt upright and brushed it off before pushing to standing. She immediately checked her pockets for her cell. Nothing.

There wasn't much in this area except for trees to one side and a lake to the other. No road. She would have to follow the tire tracks where they'd flattened the weeds. Wasting no time, she climbed out of the shallow grave and headed toward freedom, praying she would find someone willing to help her.

QUINT STABBED HIS fingers through his thick hair as exasperation settled in. Ree had been gone for hours with no word. Her cell phone tracked to the trash can on the street outside the downtown Dallas apartment they shared for the undercover assignment that he'd insisted they take so he could get vengeance for his former partner. As their last undercover case was wrapping up, a message had come from Dumitru asking Quint to kill the person who'd been arrested during the bust. The head of the crime ring believed

Quint was in jail alongside Vadik, a man Dumitru couldn't afford to have strike a plea bargain in exchange for giving up information. As it turned out, the text hadn't come from Dumitru. It had come from his secondhand man by the name of Lindy.

Putting Ree in danger due to Quint's personal need for revenge sat like a hot poker in his gut. She'd hinted she might be ready to retire her undercover career. The only reason she'd taken the last two assignments was to be the one to watch his back. She hadn't said it outright, but he knew it to be true.

James Grappell, the desk agent assigned to them, had been able to pinpoint the exact location of her phone. There was no good reason for Ree to drop her cell in the garbage. Quint had retrieved it and cleaned it off, and now it was sitting on the counter half-wrapped in a paper towel.

Ree was out there without a communication device. This was in connection to the case. No doubt in his mind. He had been asked to arrange for Vadik to die in jail. Since Quint's most recent cover story was that he'd been incarcerated and recently released, his connections on the inside should be strong and—at least to Lindy's thinking—difficult to tie back to Dumitru or any of his colleagues.

Quint had been beaten almost to a pulp a few weeks ago as part of a twisted initiation into Dumitru's crime ring.

His cell phone buzzed, still in his hand. The screen revealed an unknown caller. Since Quint could count on one hand the number of folks who had this number, he answered.

The familiar voice of his partner and fiancée came through the line. "Quint, it's me. Ree." Wind roared in the background, making it difficult to hear a word being said.

"Where are you?" he asked loudly in an attempt to speak over the noise as his pulse skyrocketed.

"On the highway, heading back to Dallas. I hitched a ride and borrowed a cell phone," she said, raising her voice. Being on the highway explained the wind tunnel sound.

"What happened and are you okay?" A half-dozen questions bottlenecked in his brain, each fighting to be the next one spoken out loud. A potent mix of anger and relief assaulted him. All he could allow himself to focus on was the fact she was alive.

"I'm good. I'll explain everything when I get there. Lock the doors, and don't respond to any messages from anyone until I'm back," she shouted. Her voice kept cutting out, but he picked up the gist of what she was saying. "Oh, and, Quint. Don't trust Giselle."

The line went dead.

Quint immediately opened his department-issued laptop as he made the call to Agent Grappell.

"She's safe," he said the second Grappell answered.

A sigh of relief came through the line.

"That's good news," Grappell said.

"All I know is she's on her way back to the apartment and told me to lock the door in the meantime," he relayed. "Get this. She told me not to trust Giselle."

"I was about to call you when my phone rang," Grappell stated. "Ree received a text at eleven forty-five this morning from the informant requesting a lunch meeting around the corner."

"Ree must not have been worried about it since she didn't text me to let me know before she left the apartment," Quint said. "I was in PT, trying to work my arm back into condition."

"She might have been in a hurry. Giselle made it seem urgent to get together but didn't give a reason as to why," Grappell informed him.

"Interesting," Quint said. "I guess I'll know the details as soon as she arrives."

"I'm not sure why she tossed her phone," Grappell said, sounding disturbed by the point.

"You and me both," Quint stated. "All I can think is that she didn't have a choice."

"As in someone did it for her?" Grappell asked.

"It's the only reason that comes to mind. She trusted Giselle as much as an informant can be relied on," Quint stated.

"There are tracking devices on cell phones if they're lost. When she didn't turn up, someone might have figured you would trace her whereabouts," Grappell reasoned.

"Makes sense to me," Quint said. Made him mad beyond belief that someone would kidnap her right outside their apartment building.

Quint's cell buzzed, indicating a text.

"Hold on a second," he said to Grappell before checking the screen. The message was from Lindy.

Get rid of the bastard and *she* comes home *alive*.

Quint knew exactly who was in league with Giselle now. Lindy. He returned to the call with Grappell.

"Lindy wants Vadik dead, and he knows I have contacts on the inside from my recent incarceration." Of course, Lindy didn't know the entire story had been fabricated as part of Quint and Ree's cover.

"Vadik is refusing to cooperate," Grappell told Quint. "He says we can lock him in solitary confinement for the rest of his life. Dish out any punishment we want. He said he intends to beat the rap and stay aboveground."

"Then I'll just have to pay him a visit and convince him otherwise," Quint responded. He had no idea how he was going to convince Vadik to turn state's witness and allow them to fake his death, but he would figure it out if it meant bringing justice for Tessa.

First things first. He needed to see that Ree was okay. She was the only person he cared about right now.

Chapter Two

Ree had no idea if the building was being watched, so she slipped in the back and made her way up to the apartment via the service elevator. The only thing she hated worse than tight spaces was heights. The apartment on the twenty-seventh floor of a thirty-story building was a nightmare.

As the elevator dinged, she realized she didn't have her key with her. Giselle must have taken Ree's purse along with her cell phone. Ree also recalled sounding the alarm to Quint, putting him on high alert, and telling him to lock the door.

It had been one helluva day so far. She was still picking dirt out of her hair.

Quint must have heard the elevator and then checked the peephole, because she'd barely taken two steps into the hallway when he flung their door open and made a straight line to her. She crashed into him at the halfway mark, then buried her face in his chest as he walked them into the apartment before closing and locking the door.

His hands cupped her face. She blinked up at him.

"They buried me," she said, fighting the emotion trying to take over at the thought of never seeing him again.

Anger flashed in his blue eyes, and his jaw muscles clenched. "They better never touch you again. We can make an excuse to get you out of here. Say one of your family members is sick and you had to go."

"They'll see it as weakness," she reminded him. "It'll hurt the case."

He thumbed a loose tendril of hair off her face.

"I don't care, Ree," he said with an overwhelming intensity that became its own physical presence. "I can't lose you."

Those words hit her with the force of a tsunami. Neither of them could predict what would happen next. Neither could guarantee this case wouldn't go south. Neither could guarantee they would both walk away in one piece.

"Let's take ourselves off the case together," she said, knowing full well he wouldn't take her up on the offer but suggesting it anyway.

Quint didn't respond. When she pulled back and looked into his eyes, she understood why. A storm brewed behind those sapphire-blues, crystalizing them, sending fiery streaks to contrast against the whites. Those babies were the equivalent of a raging wildfire that would be impossible to put out or contain. People said eyes were the window to the soul. In Quint's case, they seemed the window to his heart.

He pressed his forehead against hers and took in

an audible breath. When he exhaled, it was like he was releasing all his pent-up frustration and fear. In that moment, she understood the gravity of what he'd been going through while she'd been gone. Kidnapped. For all he knew, left for dead.

So she didn't speak either. Instead, she leaned into their connection, a connection that tethered them as an electrical current ran through her to him and back. For a split second, it was impossible to determine where he ended and she began.

Ree had no idea how long they stood there in the entryway of the apartment as though frozen in time. She didn't care. She was safe. She was home. And in that moment, she realized home was anywhere Quint was. No, she wouldn't walk away from the case, and neither would he.

Quint finally spoke first. "You must be starving and I'd like to know exactly what happened."

"I got a text from Giselle asking if I could meet her for lunch. I stepped onto the sidewalk, and a guy came out of nowhere. I was struck and the next thing I knew a rag came over my mouth. There was some kind of chemical smell that knocked me right out," she said as he walked her over to the nearest stool where she perched. "I woke up in the middle of nowhere inside a coffin to the sound of Giselle telling Lindy not to bury me alive."

Quint muttered a string of curses low and under his breath but loud enough for her to hear. "That sonofabitch."

"I'm here now," she reassured. "I'm alive and doing fine. Tired and dirty, but I'll live."

Tension radiated off Quint in waves.

"It should have been me," he ground out.

"It's over now," she said.

"I thought I lost you," he said as a mix of anger and intense sadness passed behind his eyes.

All Ree could do in that moment was lean into him as he embraced her again.

"What sounds good to you right now?" he asked after a few moments of silence.

Exhaustion set in. The only word she could say was, "Shower."

He gave a slight nod and then walked beside her to the bathroom.

"I'll have food and coffee ready when you get out." He feathered a kiss on her lips, her chin, and the base of her neck, where her pulse thumped.

Ree gave his hand a squeeze of acknowledgment before heading into the bathroom, needing to wash the dirt off her. An involuntary shiver rocked her body, thinking about being locked inside the coffin. Her hands fisted at her sides at the thought of seeing Giselle again. Ree didn't want to be in the same room with the woman. It wouldn't turn out well for Axel's girlfriend.

A shower went a long way toward making Ree feel human again. She spent another ten minutes picking splinters out of her skin where it had been exposed to the wood. The smell of fresh-brewed coffee caused her to speed up. By the time she threw on a bathrobe and sat at the bar counter, Quint was setting a plate in front of her. An omelet with the works: spinach, cheese and chives. There was toast with a smattering of jelly along with a side of fresh greens and a slice of tomato. The meal tasted as good as it smelled, and she wolfed it down in a matter of minutes.

"More?" Quint asked as he plated his own food.

"I couldn't eat another bite. Believe me, I was full halfway through." She smiled and meant it. At least she would be fine after a cup of coffee and a minute to shake off the horror of what had just happened. Quint would be recovering from his injuries for weeks if not months after what Vadik's men had done to him in the back alley of the building where Vadik lived.

"He won't cooperate," Quint informed him. "We can't make a move without his help. It's the reason you were kidnapped. They were trying to force my hand, and I can't fake his murder without his consent."

"I should have known better than to trust Giselle," Ree stated, furious with herself for the slip that could have cost her her life.

"Every agent makes mistakes, Ree," he said in a soothing tone. "Including the best like you. The trick is to not make one that leads to something permanent." He didn't say the word *death*, but it was implied. The storm brewed again. This time, he was thinking about Tessa and her unborn child.

"Did he say why?" she asked, redirecting the

subject, not yet ready to let herself off the hook. No one was perfect. She was very aware of the fact. She was also reaching a point in life where she wanted to sit out on her back porch, drink coffee and watch the sunrise. Maybe while looking after a kiddo or two.

If someone had told Ree six months ago that she'd be pining for a family, she would have laughed in their face. What was so different in her life now? *Quint*, a little voice in the back of her mind stated.

Ree shoved the thought aside and watched the man she was crazy about finish chewing the bite of food in his mouth.

"Wants to stay aboveground when he beats the rap," he informed her.

She must have made quite the face, because Quint cracked a smile.

"I know. He won't. Funny how he doesn't seem to realize it," he said.

"To each his own, I guess," she said with a shrug. "We'll have to find another way to convince him."

"I told Grappell we'd like to pay Vadik a visit," Quint said.

"That's risky," she immediately pointed out. "We're still undercover. He could blow everything for us."

"It might be a chance we have to take," Quint reasoned. "Hear me out before you tell me that I've lost it."

She nodded before picking up her coffee mug and taking a sip. Instead of setting it down on the table, she rolled the warm mug around in her hands. There wasn't much that could convince her to walk into Vadik's cell and announce herself as Ree Sheppard.

"EXPOSING OUR IDENTITIES to Vadik might validate that we know how to pull off an undercover operation. Gaining his trust is more than half the battle. When he realizes we pulled the wool over his eyes and everyone around him, he might agree," Quint stated before putting a hand up, palm out, in the surrender position. Being left wondering about Ree, the sickness in the pit of his stomach that something might have happened to her, had his wheels turning. "I do realize what that means, and if I had to pull us off the case, I would."

He was considering making the request anyway. This investigation had bad mojo wrapped around it from the start. For months, he'd been stewing and plotting his revenge. It was so close now he could almost taste it. But putting Ree's life on the line to follow through with his plans held little appeal if it meant hurting or —heaven forbid—losing her.

Reality said she could walk across the street and be hit by a car tomorrow. No one knew how long they had with someone. The thought might be sobering, but it was also true. Sickness could strike at any moment. A freak accident could take her away.

He could live with those things happening. There would be no choice. He would be gutted, and he highly doubted he would ever get over the loss, but he would know in the bottom of his heart that he'd done nothing to cause it.

Keeping her on the case was another story altogether.

"Here's what I'm thinking," he said. "We walk away now, and it'll be hell for anyone else to step in. All the work we've done up to this point is a wash. Sure, a couple more bastards are behind bars. That's a good thing. Tessa and her baby are still dead, and the reason is still walking around out there, getting away with it, thinking he's slick as they come."

Ree nodded before taking another sip of coffee. She chewed on the inside of her cheek, which told him she was not only listening but agreeing with his analysis.

"Without Vadik's cooperation, we lose our in and our window of opportunity," he continued.

She did the cheek thing again as she studied the rim of her mug.

"So, what if we go in and tell him exactly who we are and what we've been able to accomplish so far?" he asked.

"It could backfire," she said after a thoughtful pause.

"Or possibly work," he pointed out.

"And what if he doesn't decide to cooperate?" she asked. "As much as I want to throat-punch Giselle the next time I see her—and believe me when I say I haven't made up my mind just yet that I won't— she'll be dead for certain. It would be signing her death warrant along with Axel's and his family's should his family ever surface again."

"You're right," he admitted. "There is a whole lot that can go wrong with this plan. But we're short on options."

"This is a dangerous Hail Mary," she reasoned. "There's a whole lot on the line if the meeting doesn't go well."

"Very true," he agreed. "Axel's family is in WIT-SEC. It's not a guarantee no one will ever find them, but the US Marshals office has a long and successful track record of keeping their witnesses safe. Axel refuses to go in until Giselle and his son are safe."

"I agree. I have a whole lot of respect for the agency," she concurred.

"Giselle is a wild card," he admitted.

"Truer words have never been spoken," Ree said. "I thought she was pining for Axel and wishing he would get out of prison so her son would know his father. When we first met, she seemed like she wished the three of them could be a family. After spending time with her, I realize she has a very loose definition of what a family looks like."

Quint nodded. He also realized there was more to the story there, but he didn't want to derail the conversation by asking questions.

"Plus, I think she's so used to the penthouse life and being taken care of by the others that it doesn't even seem to bother her much that her son lives with her sister," Ree continued. "I bought the sad act at first. But seeing her in action at the penthouse, I'm not sure she wants the role of full-time mother."

"There are plenty of strong single women out

there kicking butt and taking names," he stated. He should know. His own mother had been one of them. She'd worked two jobs to keep food on the table. They'd lived in a trailer park on the outskirts of Houston, and she'd been gone most of the time, working. Quint had been young and stupid. He got bored. Lonely. So he ended up getting into trouble when he should have been studying his backside off and picking up the slack at home. One of the times Quint got into trouble, the liaison officer at his school stepped in, realizing Quint needed a male role model in his life. Officer Jazz had been a lifesaver. He took it upon himself to speak to the school. Quint's teachers apparently came forward saying he used to be a good student and they weren't sure what happened. Jazzy, as he used to call him, didn't leave it there. He kept digging and then eventually asked if he could sit with Quint at lunch one day. Said he would like to be Quint's sponsor in a mentoring program. Quint had balked at first, but then he got into a real fix. He distinctly remembered the day he'd sat across the dining room table from his mom and saw the exhaustion and hurt in her eyes. She could barely stay awake because she'd worked all night at the hospital, changing bedpans. In that moment, it had clicked. Quint realized his mother deserved so much better from him.

The word *saint* didn't begin to cover it when it came to his mother. She sure didn't deserve to get sick and die before he could repay her for all the amazing things she'd given him and done for him growing up. Anger welled inside him as he thought about how his father had walked away from the mother of his child, not to mention the child itself. Taking in a slow breath, he flexed and released his fingers a couple of times to work out some of the tension that came with the memories.

Ree had been the first person he'd opened up to about his mother. He'd never even spoken about her to Tessa, and the two of them had been best friends. Sharing a part of his life with Ree no one else knew about and wanting to show her the small things made him realize she was different, special.

"I don't get the impression Giselle could ever be confused with being a strong woman," Ree stated with a little ire in her tone. She had every right to be angry.

"Nope," he agreed.

A visible tremor rocked Ree.

"What is it?" he asked. "Tell me what happened to you and exactly how Giselle was involved."

Chapter Three

Ree recounted the story of getting a last-minute text, practically sprinting out the door and then being kidnapped literally the minute she walked onto the street. It was broad daylight. Giselle was making a beeline toward Ree, waving. Two guys flanked her. It had all happened so fast, in spite of the fact Ree was trained to check her surroundings for clues.

The whole incident sounded like something out of a spy movie, even to her.

"These situations are rehearsed. They're good at what they do," she stated, even more frustrated someone had gotten the drop on her. She was skilled at her job too. There was no reason she should have been caught unawares. Of course, she'd learned to go with the flow a long time ago in her law enforcement career. Being undercover for the past two years had honed the lesson. As awful as these incidents could be, they often led to a break in a case. *Or a body bag one day*, she thought.

"There's a reason this ring is one of, if not *the* best weapons trafficking ring in North America,"

Quint said. The comment was most likely meant to ease her embarrassment at allowing herself to fall into their trap, even though the statement was true. "And letting them kidnap you was your best chance at staying alive."

Quint seemed just as upset about what she'd been through as she was. If the shoe was on the other foot, she would be frantic too.

"After they buried me in the coffin-like crate, they shoveled dirt on top," she said, pausing as the memory caused her chest to tighten. She released the breath she'd been holding. "Giselle came to my rescue. She begged Lindy to stop what he was doing and at least give me a chance to breathe."

"That was good of her, considering she was the one who betrayed you in the first place." His tone held the same rage she was experiencing.

"My thoughts exactly," she quipped. "But I have to give her props for going to bat for me. He would have buried me all the way if she hadn't stepped in, and her intervention is probably the reason I was able to push through and open the top. Otherwise, the weight might have been too heavy, and there might not have been any give."

Her body shuddered involuntarily at the thought.

"I'll kill that bastard," Quint managed to grind out. Except they both knew he wouldn't. Not if he wanted to keep his job, his pension and his self-respect.

"At least he stopped, or I might still be buried," she said with another shiver. "He said something about coming back for me if I stayed alive. I'm guessing he reached out to you shortly after to force your hand into ensuring Vadik is dead."

"Lindy planned to leave you there overnight?" Quint said. Again the jaw muscle pulsed.

"Seems so," she admitted, not real thrilled with the idea either. "At least he planned to come back. Plus, we have his timeline. For all he knows, I'm still out there buried alive."

"He was the one who reached out to say I needed to get rid of Vadik in the text message," he reminded.

"We could get him on solicitation of murder," she explained. "He would go away for a very long time on a charge like that one."

Quint nodded even though he knew as well as she did there was no way they would go through with it. Not when they could get Dumitru instead.

"That about sums up my side," she said.

"Have you made up your mind about whether or not you think we should pay Vadik a visit?" he asked.

"Are you asking my permission?" She didn't bother to hide the shock in her voice. She wasn't trying to be a jerk. He actually caught her off guard.

"No," he said, hesitating for a few seconds. Then came, "We both know this investigation wouldn't be where it is without you. We make a great undercover team." He paused for a few beats. "But I think our relationship outside of work is the most important one. At least, it is to me."

"You won't get any argument from me there," she agreed, and meant it with all her heart.

He reached over and covered her hand with his.

The connection calmed her nerves a notch below panic as she relived the horrible day and the decision they needed to make about Vadik.

"If he doesn't agree, we walk away, and he gets locked up in solitary confinement," Quint continued.

"What about the case, Quint?" she asked. "Will you be able to leave it behind? You have a whole lot of history behind this one and a personal connection binding you to the outcome. Knowing you as well as I do, I find it difficult to believe you'll be able to move on without getting the closure you deserve."

Quint sat there for a long moment without saying a word. With his free hand, he took a few sips of coffee before setting the mug down near hers.

"I can't make any promises, because I don't know how I'll feel if the lead dries up," he started. "There are a whole lot of things I want to say, and believe. But you're right. I would be naive to think losing out on Dumitru after being this close wouldn't eat me alive from the inside out."

She nodded. They weren't the words she wanted to hear, but they were brutally honest.

"Then there's you to consider." He brought her hand up to his lips and placed a tender kiss on the inside of her wrist. "I've never had anyone in my life before who makes me want to come home every night. There hasn't been anyone I couldn't walk away from and get over like that." He snapped his fingers. "Until you."

"How does that change the investigation?" she asked, her body literally warming. This close, she could breathe in his spicy male scent. She'd memorized it...*him*.

"I still want to lock Dumitru behind bars and throw away the key," he admitted, the fire back and dancing in his eyes. "Make no mistake about it."

Quint took in a breath, and then slowly released it.

"But I plan to come home to you every day for the rest of our lives," he said. "And this case won't... *can't*...be the reason I don't get to."

"I want out, Quint," she stated, unsure of how he was going to react to what she had to say next. "This job. This life." She brought her eyes up to meet his. "It isn't a life, but it does overtake one."

"If you're happy, that's all I need to hear," he said. "I love you, Ree. I want to spend the rest of our lives together. I don't care what you do for a living. What we have between us is the only priority for me."

Ree took in another deep breath. Why was it so difficult for her to admit what she needed to tell him? She'd said yes when he'd asked her to marry him. He was her best friend and her everything. Shouldn't telling him be easy?

"What is it, Ree?" A look of concern darkened those stormy blue eyes.

"There's something I need to tell you," she said.

"Okay," he responded, squaring his shoulders like he was preparing to take a punch.

"I'm not sure if what I have to say will change how you feel about me in any way," she continued, searching for the right words, the right moment to speak what had been on her mind.

"You can tell me anything," he said, his brow furrowing.

Since there was no easy way to say it, she decided to go for it.

"I want kids."

Quint's jaw dropped, and she panicked.

"IT DOESN'T HAVE to be right away." Ree qualified her statement—a statement that had thrown Quint for a loop.

"Okay," he said, trying to process the fact they'd shifted gears into unknown territory.

"Okay?" she asked.

Quint wasn't sure how he felt about the idea. To be honest, he'd never given kids serious consideration. His life had felt lacking in a strange way recently. He'd tried to chalk it up to losing Tessa, but the feeling had been there for much longer than the past eight or nine months. He'd been restless before his partner had died and long before Ree came along. He was still trying to sort out what it all meant.

"We've been tied up with the case, so I've been focused on that recently," he said by way of explanation. The tiny muscles in her face tensed as he spoke, and he realized he was disappointing her with his response. An apology seemed in order. Except that he really didn't know where he stood on kids. Quint was certain where he *used* to stand on the subject. But a lot had changed since meeting Ree. He'd never thought he'd be eager to spend the rest of his life with someone until her.

"Forget I said anything," she quickly backpedaled. "It's too soon anyway."

It wasn't, though. He was in his forties. She was four years shy of her fortieth birthday. If they wanted kids, they probably should be thinking about them, making plans. Under normal circumstances, the idea would have made Quint's brain explode. Surprisingly enough, it didn't.

"I'd like to put the subject on hold for now," he said, and noticed the tension lines forming on her face. "Just until we figure out if we're off this case or moving full steam ahead. Okay?"

"Makes sense. We should visit Vadik," she said, but the enthusiasm was gone from her eyes. "We have plenty of time to talk about our future."

"I'll hold off responding to Lindy until we talk to Vadik," he said, figuring he needed to fire off a text to Grappell to set everything up.

"We need to find Vadik's Achilles' heel," Ree said as Quint sent off the message to their desk agent.

"He doesn't have children or a wife. At least, not obviously. They must be tucked away somewhere if they exist," Quint said.

"I didn't see any pictures or indications there were children at the penthouse. Did you?" she asked.

"No," he responded. She'd spent more time there than him, so she would have been the one to notice.

"Vadik doesn't act married either. Although we both know the definition of marriage and relationships in their world doesn't exactly match with ours," she continued.

Quint agreed.

"I wonder if there is anyone special in his life," she said.

"It sure would make our lives a whole lot easier if we found someone to use as leverage," Quint agreed.

Ree sucked in a breath.

"What about a sibling?" she asked.

"I'll see what else Grappell found out about Vadik," Quint said. "Everything has been happening so fast, details are slipping. I should already know this."

"We're here now and we'll figure it out. I'd start with asking about bank records," she said. "See if he sends money to anyone on a regular basis who isn't connected to the crime ring."

"A money exchange like that would most likely happen under the table, or he would find a way to launder it," he said.

"True." She chewed on the inside of her cheek again. "What do we know about the guy other than the fact that he's high-ranking within Dumitru's organization?"

"That's all I have so far." Quint sent off another request for personal information about Vadik. "He seems to keep his personal life separate from his professional one."

"I don't think he lives at the penthouse full-time," she said.

"Why is that?" he asked.

"It's a party spot, and when I went seeking out a bathroom once, I ended up in the master bedroom. It was a basic room. There wasn't anything personal in there. I ducked inside and checked the drawers and closet. Same thing. There was very little in the way of clothing, and I almost tripped over a weekender bag sitting next to the door."

"Interesting," Quint stated, hoping this meant Grappell would be able to dig up usable information on the man. Right now, all they had to use as incentive was negotiating for a lighter sentence. With a hotshot lawyer, the case against Vadik could get kicked out of court. The thought sent fire racing through Quint.

Criminals shouldn't get to roam the streets or do whatever they wanted because they had enough money to pay for the best lawyers. Don't even get him started on the ones who were part of human trafficking organizations. Vadik needed to rot in jail for his part. Quint might have jeopardized their last case by calling the bust early, but it had been worth it.

"Speaking of Vadik," Ree started. "Did Grappell update the file about the kids?"

"Yes," he said. He'd been forced to end the last case earlier than he would have liked when half a dozen kids were brought to Vadik's jewelry store along with trunks full of weapons. There'd been no way Quint could walk away from the scene and allow those children to be sold. Period.

The move had cost him valuable time that he needed to build a strong case against Vadik while working his way to Dumitru. Seeing the look in those kids' eyes had caused him to snap. All he'd been able to think about was Tessa's unborn baby and what she would have thought of him if he'd allowed children to be sold. Children he had the power to help.

So he'd done what he had to and called for the raid. He'd made a point of slipping out, getting away, and outrunning the cops who'd shown up to make the arrests. One of Vadik's colleagues had set the building on fire, destroying valuable evidence.

The case against Vadik wasn't strong, and he seemed to realize it. Gaining his cooperation without the right leverage was going to be an uphill battle. But all the cards had been played, and this was the only hope.

"She would be proud of you. You know that, right?" Ree said, breaking into his reverie.

"How do you know I was thinking about Tessa?" he asked.

"You get a look on your face," she said with a shrug. "I noticed."

"I hope she would be proud," was all he said.

"We've gone in with nothing before and come out with what we needed," Ree continued. "We make a good team."

"No arguments there," Quint agreed. So much so, he could barely imagine doing this job without her as his partner. His cell buzzed, so he checked the screen. The message was from Grappell.

"What is it?" Ree asked.

"I think we just got our leverage," Quint said, placing a call to their desk agent.

Chapter Four

"Vadik has a mother."

"I'm guessing there's more to this announcement," Ree said, considering everyone had a mom. "Even creeps like him had to come from somewhere."

"True enough. He keeps her tucked away, though," Agent Grappell continued.

"With the circles he runs in, I don't blame him for keeping his mother far away from his day-to-day life," Quint stated.

"Why not keep her at his place, though?" Ree asked, figuring the man had enough money to put security around his mother twenty-four-seven. His penthouse had more guns than a shooting range on half-price day.

"She needs full-time care," Grappell explained. "Her memory is failing, and she has health issues. He keeps her in a pricey place overlooking Lake Travis in hill country. Believe me when I say that I had to dig deep to get this information."

Ree involuntarily shivered at a couple of those words: *dig deep*. The image of the box she'd been buried in came to mind. Try as she might, shaking off the feeling that her chest was caving in was hard. She reminded herself where she was, in the apartment, safe with Quint.

Why did they have to bury her? The *one* thing she would have the most difficult time recovering from was her claustrophobia.

Glancing down in her lap, she realized she'd subconsciously twisted her fingers together. Flexing and releasing her fingers a few times served to work off some of the tension. A couple of deep breaths later and she felt half-human again. Confronting Giselle was something Ree looked forward to. *If* she got to the woman first. Quint seemed ready to pounce the minute they laid eyes on her. A little voice in the back of Ree's mind picked that moment to remind her she wouldn't be sitting here right now if not for Giselle's intervention. The thought helped dial down the heat boiling in Ree's veins.

Grappell rattled off the address of the group home where Vadik's mother lived as Ree clued back into the conversation.

"There are only four residents in the McMansion on the hillside," Grappell continued. "There's twice as many staff as residents. There's a cook dedicated to fixing nutritious meals."

"I imagine security will be tight," Quint stated with a glance toward Ree. He sat close to her, like he didn't want her farther away than arm's reach. There was something about his physical presence that reassured her too. Like somehow life would always work out if the two of them were connected, together.

"True," Ree agreed.

"I'll see what I can do about getting the layout of the residence and the property," Grappell stated. "I'm guessing you'll want to act as soon as possible on the mother."

"If we have her, we have leverage," Quint said. "Without her, we don't have a leg to stand on."

"Vadik doesn't seem like he'll cooperate otherwise," Grappell agreed. "What are we talking about here? Removing his mother from her environment could backfire considering she needs medical care."

"Maybe we don't have to take her anywhere," Ree piped up. "Can we send in a drone and get some pictures of her on the lawn? Maybe snap a few of her in her room from the window? All we need is to see from the outside looking in and we'll have something to show Vadik. A threat to his mother would work."

"I could fake documents saying we're going to deport her," Grappell said.

"That should shake him up quite a bit," she agreed. "He must want her close to him rather than halfway around the world."

Quint was nodding, and she could practically see the wheels turning.

"How long before you can get those printouts to us?" he asked.

"A couple of hours for the digital files," Grappell stated. "A couple more for the prints."

"We can go in with pictures on our cell phones," Ree said. "All we're trying to do is shake the man up."

"Darn," Quint protested. "I like the idea of slamming a file folder down on the table with photos in it."

Ree smiled for the second time that day. Only Quint could bring out her lighter side after the day she'd had.

"Why don't you guys hunker down for the rest of tonight and let me work on this?" Grappell asked.

"I don't know," Ree started. "A middle-of-the-night visit, being yanked out of the comfort of his bed, might be just what he needs to wake up and realize we're offering him his only choice out of the mess he's made of his life."

"If his mother's health is on the line, he might not care about anything else," Quint pointed out.

"That's why we have to convince him to help us," Ree continued. "Without us, his mother gets deported, and there's no one there to take care of her. She gets sicker. Maybe even dies while he rots in a cell." Ree snapped her fingers. "If he cooperates, we don't touch her. It's that simple."

Quint was nodding in agreement.

"It's our best bet," Grappell stated. "I'll send the drone and see if we can capture any shots of dear old mom."

"Thank you," Ree said, figuring Grappell didn't get near enough credit for everything he did for investigations like this one. He'd been their assigned agent on four cases now, all of which were leading up to Dumitru's eventual capture. At least, Ree hoped they would be able to incarcerate the man responsible for Tessa's death. Otherwise, Ree's fiancé might live in a mental prison of his own making for the rest of his life.

THEY HAD A solid lead. Quint should be happy. And yet what had happened to Ree still had him shaken up to the point he wasn't sure it was worth going on with the investigation. But stopping now wasn't an option either. Ree wouldn't want him to walk away at this point over her. She was fully capable of doing her job, and she had been doing just that this afternoon at lunchtime when she'd been abducted off the street in front of their apartment building.

Lindy was flexing, showing he could do whatever he wanted, whenever he wanted, and no one—not even Quint—would be able to stop the man. Lindy was essentially telling Quint that he could take his girlfriend in broad daylight and there wasn't squat Quint could do about it. His hand involuntarily fisted as they ended the call with Grappell. The desk agent had promised to let them know the minute he had any pictures to work with. Those pictures were going to sway Vadik into agreeing to cooperate. *They had to.*

"Hey, are you doing all right?" Ree's voice traveled over to him. He looked up at her and realized she'd been studying him. He shouldn't be surprised at this point. She seemed to be able to read his moods.

"I can't help but think I let you down today," he admitted.

"You didn't," she argued.

"If I'd been downstairs with you then—"

Ree put a hand up to stop him.

"Quint, you would step in front of a bullet for me. Don't be so hard on yourself considering you can't physically be around every second. Plus, I'm a qualified agent," she pointed out.

"You're right up there with the best I've ever worked with or come across professionally. And that's saying a whole lot," he agreed. Still, risking her life felt like the most selfish thing he would ever do. Tessa would kick his behind if she was alive. Somewhere deep down, he realized she wouldn't want him going after the guy connected to the case. So why couldn't he let it go?

The thought of walking away from this case and from his job had never appealed. He hadn't given a whole lot of thought to what he would do when he was finished putting his life on the line. Had he ever seriously considered retiring? A voice tucked in the back of his minds pointed out the fact that he never really expected to live long enough to retire.

Until Ree, he didn't have much to live for. The realization struck like stray lightning on a sunny day. Now he had someone to build a future with who felt the same. He was still figuring out kids. He'd never given them much consideration at all until Tessa had turned up pregnant, and then he'd been focused on being the stand-in dad her kiddo would need. Not once did he truly consider becoming a biological father. Ree's comment had thrown him off guard before, and he was still regaining his balance. Did he want kids?

The question had to be shelved for now. This wasn't the right time or place. Besides, all he could think about was putting Dumitru behind bars and this case in the rearview once and for all. Tessa would want him to move on. This was the only way he could sleep at night.

"Quint?" Ree's voice broke in.

"Yes," he responded.

"Where did you go just now?" she asked, still studying him.

He hoped she wasn't worried about what she'd gotten herself into by saying yes when he'd proposed.

"I'm all over the place," he admitted. "Mainly, I'm determined to wrap this case up as quickly as possible so we can move forward with life."

"I'd drink to that," she said with a warm smile. "Since you're already bouncing topics, where do you want to live after the wedding?"

"I guess I hadn't thought too much about it," he admitted. Honestly, he hadn't gotten much further than ending the case. "Where would you like to live?"

"I'd been assuming that we would live at my place, but that's not exactly fair to you," she said.

He reached over and took her hand in his. Physical contact with Ree had a way of calming the always raging storm inside him.

"I want to live wherever you are. My place isn't big enough for the two of us. I love your grounds.

Moving into your home, making it ours, sounds right to me," he said.

"Are you serious?" she asked. "Because I would love that too."

"Then it's decided," he stated. "Besides, I want you to be closer to your family."

"That means a lot to me, Quint," she said. Then came a cheeky smile. "But you may live to regret it. You've met them. My mom isn't going to welcome you with open arms."

"She will if we tell her that I'm the reason you're planning on leaving undercover work," he teased.

Ree laughed, and she had a musical quality to her voice.

"You'll get even more brownie points if you tell her you put your foot down," she said with an eye roll.

He shook his head.

"I can't imagine a reason in the world your mother wouldn't be bursting with pride every time she thought about you," he said in all seriousness. "Not only are you one of the best undercover agents I've had the pleasure of working with, but you're a good person to boot. You're intelligent, quick-witted, and can hold your own. I have yet to see you back down from anyone or anything."

"That's the problem right there," she said. "My mother wanted a girlie-girl, and that has never been me."

"She is missing out on an incredible daughter," he stated. "If we ever have a girl, I hope she is just like you."

Ree shot him a look as he heard the words coming out of his own mouth. Shock didn't begin to describe his reaction to what he'd just said. She seemed to catch on to the fact he'd just spoken without thinking and clamped her mouth shut.

A text came through, breaking into the moment. Quint checked the screen. "Grappell doesn't quite have the photos of Vadik's mother yet, but he says we might not need them. As soon as Vadik's mother was mentioned, he backpedaled and said he might be ready to talk."

"That's good." She pushed to standing. "We should go strike while the iron is hot."

Quint suppressed the urge to ask her to stay in the apartment, reminding himself she was a more than capable undercover agent. Being in love with her was like having his heart walking around outside of his chest. If he loved and wanted to protect her this way, he couldn't imagine how much more that would extend to their children.

Was he seriously considering a family?

Ree deserved to have everything she wanted, and that seemed to include little rug rats running around. Could he give that to her? Did he really have a choice? He would do anything to make her happy. Now he needed to figure out how to be just as enthusiastic at the thought as she seemed to be.

Quint grabbed the keys from the counter and then tucked his cell phone inside his back pocket.

"Give me one second to get dressed," she said before grabbing clothes and then disappearing into the bathroom. She emerged a couple of minutes later.

He walked Ree out of the apartment, to the elevator and then to the waiting SUV with his hand on the small of her back.

After surveying the parking lot, she climbed inside the vehicle. The way her jaw was set and her gaze narrowed told him she was still reeling from being kidnapped this morning. The same had happened to him, except the part about being stuffed inside a makeshift coffin. Every undercover agent who'd been on the job longer than a few years had, at one time, been abducted or lured to a questionable place in the name of a case. Quint was going to have to figure out a way to get past the fact it had happened to Ree despite how much his protective instincts flared. Besides, their future family didn't work without her.

Chapter Five

The ride to the Dallas County Corrections Department was quiet. Between the coffin and talking to Quint about possibly having babies in the future, a lot of ground had been covered. Becoming an undercover agent two years ago was the pinnacle of a hard-fought career, but the job had become her life. Preston, her ex-boyfriend who also happened to be her older brother's best friend, and her family had been right all along. The only thing she'd cared about up to this point was work. What they were missing was the fact she'd never met anyone before who made her want to consider another path.

Quint Casey was the difference. But now she needed to refocus on what they were going to say to Vadik and how the next steps of their plan might fall into place. *The sooner the better* came to mind when she thought about wrapping this one up. It was also the first time in her career that she'd followed a target over four undercover operations. The longer the two of them stayed with this, the more dangerous it became. The risk of their identity being uncovered grew with each passing day.

Quint parked the Chevy Blazer in the lot but didn't immediately exit the vehicle. He sat there, staring out the windshield, looking like he had something to say. His lips formed a grim line.

After releasing a sharp sigh, he asked, "Ready?"

This was it, she realized. After securing Vadik's help, they would enter the final steps of what had been a very long journey so far. And if they couldn't get Vadik's agreement, if this was some sort of trick to get them down here so he could spit in their faces, Quint and Ree would have to step out of the case and back into their lives. They had a wedding to look forward to and a real future. She worried it wouldn't be enough if her fiancé didn't get closure. They'd come this far. Failure wouldn't be an option to Quint no matter how often he'd said he could walk away. There'd been no conviction in his words, and she couldn't allow him to compromise or he could end up bitter. There was no way she could live with herself if she was the reason he stopped working on Tessa's case.

The desk sergeant escorted the two of them to a small room with a table and three chairs. He locked the door behind them and then disappeared. Quint tapped his finger on the tabletop as they waited. After what seemed like forever but was more like fifteen minutes, an officer brought Vadik into the room through a door on the opposite side of the room, deposited him and then indicated he would be waiting on the other side of the door.

Vadik Gajov was five-feet-nine to five-feet-ten, if Ree had to guess. He would be considered average height by European standards. Here in Dallas, he stuck out as being short.

"Have a seat, Vadik," Quint said. His gaze narrowed, and his tone left no room for doubt that he wasn't there to play.

"I like to stand." Vadik had a thick eastern European accent. His intense gray eyes settled on Ree.

Instinctively, Quint stood up, drawing attention back to himself. "Then we'll both stand."

This was a contest to see who could claim to be in control of this conversation. Vadik had already lost. She could tell from his slight pout that he was unaccustomed to be on the losing side of any matchup. Too bad. He was already behind the eight ball, and the reality he had a mother to protect put him securely at their mercy.

"Do what you want," Vadik said, crossing his arms. "Now that I know you're both cops, what do you really want?" A look of disdain radiated from dark eyes. His gaze lingered on Ree for a few seconds and his top lip curled in what looked like a growl. "You?"

"That's right. And I'm an agent not a cop. You'll get a lot further with us if you cooperate," she stated, unfazed by his reaction.

He sat there for a long moment, staring her down.

"You already know what we want. Your cooperation." Quint shifted the focus to him.

"In return for what?" Vadik asked. "What will you do for me?"

"Allow your mother to stay in the country, for one," Quint said calmly, like he was reading the Sunday paper in his house slippers with a cup of coffee nearby.

"Fine," Vadik said, brushing nonexistent lint off the sleeve of his orange jumpsuit like he had all day. "What else?"

"That's the only thing I can promise," Quint stated. "And that's pushing it."

"What if I don't agree to your terms?" Vadik asked.

"Then dear old mom gets deported and is never allowed back in the US," Quint said. "I bet you have some relatives back home who would be willing to take her in and care for her. Right, Vadik?"

He bristled and recovered almost as quickly. As much as he was trying to play his cards close to the vest, he had no power here. Still, his pride seemed like it would hold him back as much as possible.

"I'll be honest with you. Keeping my mother in this country is my greatest wish," Vadik said. "However, never being able to see her again is a knife to the chest."

Ree observed the tension lines in Vadik's forehead. She saw the deep grooves around his mouth that hadn't been there before.

"I understand," Quint said, not offering to go to bat for Vadik.

"They will kill me," Vadik said. Ree glanced at

his hands and realized he'd been chewing his finger-nails to the quick. The cool, penthouse-living, suit-wearing image was a far cry from the man standing in front of her now.

"They are already trying," Quint stated. "They sent me to get it done because they have no idea about my true identity. Otherwise, you'd already be dead instead of sitting in this room talking to us."

Vadik audibly gasped. "It makes no sense why they would come after me this way."

His shoulders deflated despite his chin shooting up.

"You're too close to Dumitru," Quint pointed out. "He doesn't want to risk you talking to save your own hide."

"He should know that I would never do that." Va-dik's grip on his arms caused his knuckles to turn white.

"Law enforcement is circling, Vadik. He has to know some of his men, especially the ones closest to him, might turn," Quint pointed out.

Ree stayed quiet up to this point. Mainly because Vadik might love his mother, but he didn't respect women. She'd seen the way he treated them at the penthouse, not allowing them to stand at the bar be-cause it cheapened them in his eyes. The women there were nothing more than party girls to be dis-posed of when they were deemed too old or no lon-ger useful. It made Ree sick to her stomach thinking about the manner in which Vadik treated people. Looking at him now as he faced the music from a lifetime of crime, it was impossible to drum up sympathy for the man for the fact he might not see his mother again.

She did, however, feel a twinge of sadness for the elderly woman who was completely dependent on Vadik for her quality of care. Ree highly doubted any of Vadik's relatives in Romania would take her care this seriously.

There were always so many casualties in the criminal world. Ree had also seen families who knew exactly what was happening and protected their own. She assumed they were protecting their free ride since many of them lived in nice houses with no real incomes on record. Crime families had a strange dynamic, Ree thought. Her own family seemed normal by comparison, and on many levels, it was. Her mother didn't agree with Ree's career choice. Had Ree worked harder to climb the ladder out of spite? She wasn't a vengeful person, but she did push her mother's buttons at times. Now that Ree was thinking of having a family of her own, she was softening toward her mother, beginning to see a little bit of the woman's point of view.

Her mother's concern did come from a place of love and care. Ree's shoulders deflated. Had she been part of the reason for the rift? Was her brother Shane right about Ree needling her mother at the point of her insecurity?

Thinking of having a family was resetting Ree's priorities already. She could scarcely imagine what it was going to be like when she actually had kids.

Maybe it was time to give her mother a break? After all, no parent was perfect, and Ree was beginning to see how difficult the job of bringing up kids was going to be. She was already second-guessing herself in the parenting department.

And then what happened if the kid turned out to be like the thugs she put behind bars? What if she had a child just like Vadik?

Quint said he would be open to having kids. Did he realize what he might be getting into?

"If I AGREE to these terms, will I ever see my mother again?" Vadik's question was valid. It wasn't the one he needed to be asking.

"You're dead to her either way," Quint stated. All he had to do was think about the half-dozen children Vadik had been so ready to sell to the highest bidder to be able to distance any sympathy Quint might have had. He called up the dirty and scared faces of each one because he'd burned the details into his memory. "I'm offering a way your mother can stay safe and well cared for."

"Not without money," Vadik said. "The government has already seized all my assets by now. My bank accounts are most likely frozen. How will my mother be cared for if there is no money to pay the bills?"

"How far up is she paid?" Quint could have Grappell look into the details, but he wanted to see how honest Vadik would be.

"Five years," he supplied. "Give or take."

"A lot can happen in five years," Quint pointed out. He wasn't making any promises and wouldn't. The man needed to pay for his crimes. Being kind to his aging mother didn't erase his willingness to sell innocent children who'd been stripped from their families. So, no, he didn't have a whole lot of sympathy for Vadik. Don't even get Quint started on how the man treated women in general. Being kind to his own mother did nothing to purge the rest of his sins.

Vadik paced back and forth along the back wall. All pretense he was sitting in the driver's seat of the conversation was gone now. The man was in self-preservation mode. All he seemed to care about was his mother and his own fate.

"I'll beat these charges," Vadik stated. "I have access to the best lawyers through my connections."

"You could roll the dice, but the evidence against you is strong. I've seen guys like you locked away for the rest of their lives with half this much proof. Not to mention the fact I've never lost a case when I'm the star witness," Quint said. It was true. He was an excellent witness.

Vadik frowned.

"You've never gone against my lawyers," he said. "And when I get out of this hole, I intend to stay aboveground."

"You seem to be forgetting one very important point," Quint continued. "They sent *me* to kill you already. Even if you have the best lawyers in the world, you'll never make it to trial. If I don't get the job done, they'll just send someone else."

Vadik's eyebrows drew together like he was trying to figure out how to split an atom.

"Then there's the obvious fact the government seized all your assets, and all your accounts are frozen, which is a long-winded way of pointing out that you're broke," Quint continued. "Your former employer seems ready to cut bait."

A long, drawn-out silence sat heavy in the room.

"How would it go down?" he asked, stopping in front of the same door he'd walked through minutes ago.

"It would have to be visible," Quint figured. "Probably a fake attack in the yard or in your cell. We'll plant someone to carry it out. They'll most likely use blood-like pouches the size of washing detergent pods."

When Vadik gave Quint a sideways glance, he held out his hand palm up.

"They would fit here basically," Quint explained, motioning toward his palm and drawing the shape of an egg there. It dawned on him that a man like Vadik wouldn't know how to use a washer or dryer. The guy probably hadn't lifted a finger since rising in the ranks of A-12, the organization headed by Dumitru.

"And what would that do?" Vadik's eyebrows drew together, and his lips thinned. He didn't like what he was hearing, but he was listening intently. Quint could work with that.

"Cause a burst of what looks like blood. The attacker can fit it in the palm of his hand, so when he shows a knife or sharp object, everyone will assume the blood is from you," Quint said. "It'll splatter all over you and the person attacking you, which makes it all the more believable to bystanders."

"What about others? Some might join in," Vadik said. "Try to get in a punch or a stab."

"This has to look natural but will be tightly controlled to ensure that doesn't happen." Quint noticed how careful Vadik was being while placing himself in harm's way. His thoughts snapped back to the kids at Vadik's store. Quint reminded himself to exhale. The notion of bringing kids into a world with people like Vadik running around didn't sit well. Of course, he did realize many of the kids who were kidnapped came from vulnerable situations at home. Alcoholic or neglectful parents, or both, who weren't paying attention put their kids most at risk. Then there were the older kids who ran away thinking they could get a better deal on the streets than in their own homes. Ree and Quint's children would have two parents who stuck around, provided for them and loved them.

His mind snapped to Ree's father. He'd been killed on the job while working law enforcement. Quint had toyed around with the idea of walking away from the job recently. Could he?

The last thing he wanted was to be the kind of father who disappeared for weeks on end, leaving his wife and children to worry about whether or not he was coming home. Since Tessa and her baby's death, being an undercover agent had been losing its shine anyway. What would Quint do if he left the only career he'd ever known?

"And all this is for show?" Vadik asked, interrupting Quint's thoughts. Did the man seriously believe a federal agent would set up a fake death and then actually kill him? Vadik seemed to be getting the idea of the scrutiny agents were under to do their jobs. He had to account for every bullet fired, and not just for inventory purposes. The bullet had to be traced and explained once it struck.

"It is," Quint confirmed, figuring this wasn't the time to educate Vadik on policy. "You might be struck, possibly bruised, so a lawyer will come in the room after we're finished here to explain your legal rights."

"And there's no plea bargain on the table for me?" Vadik had the boldness to ask.

All Quint had to do in order to answer that question was think about having kids of his own, or any of the many other children already born who Vadik would sell if he had a chance when he walked free again.

"No. Absolutely not. There's no way my boss would approve a deal for you," he said, knowing full well he would never even consider asking for one.

"Then there's no way I'll help you," Vadik concluded. "I'm sorry to have wasted your time."

Ree flinched ever so slightly.

Quint pushed up to standing.

"Very well then. You'll be locked in solitary confinement until our case concludes so you can't speak to anyone," Quint said, as serious as the day was long.

Quint glanced at Ree, who immediately stood.

She'd been quiet so far, and he realized why. Vadik would listen to Quint more than he would a woman. It was one of Vadik's many disgusting qualities.

Ree turned to the door and took the couple of steps. Quint reached for the handle as she spun around and then folded her arms.

"Before we go," she started, and then seemed to lock onto Vadik. "What message would you like us to give your mother?"

Chapter Six

Vadik blinked a couple of times at Ree before answering. For a long moment, it seemed like he was dumbfounded by her comment.

She provoked him. "Come on, Vad. You had to know we would leave here and go straight to her. She'll be in a holding cell at immigration before you brush your teeth for bed."

He stood a little straighter but held his tongue.

"I just hope she doesn't end up with lice like the last batch we sent over there," she continued, figuring painting a vivid picture would work better than any words ever could.

"Right," Quint piped in when Vadik kept his mouth clamped. "And then some of the elderly scratched so hard they drew blood."

"It was a mess," she said with a shrug toward Vadik. "But, hey, that's no longer our problem once we get her in the system."

Ree turned toward the exit.

"Wait," Vadik finally acquiesced. His tone gave

away his intentions long before his actual words. "I'm not finished talking."

"Yes, you are," Ree said, acting unfazed. The jerk needed to sweat it a little after being stubborn from the moment they'd walked through the door.

"Hold on," Vadik said, his tone more pleading this time. Now they were getting somewhere. He sized Ree up. "I knew you were different from the others." He let his gaze wander over her. "Too bad. We could have had a good time together."

She didn't take it personally. It probably galled him to no end that he had to cower to a woman he viewed as beneath him.

"Personally, you don't do anything for me," she quipped. "But then, you never did. So if you're ready to talk about how this will play out, we'll consider sitting down again. But you'll say, 'Yes, ma'am,' when you speak to me from now on or we walk out the door."

"You would risk your precious case?" Vadik said with disdain.

"In my world, there's more than one way to skin a cat," she countered. "You are one option." She didn't bring up the fact he was the best and quickest. Information with Vadik was on a need-to-know basis.

"You will protect my mother?" Vadik asked.

"We'll ensure her safety," Ree stated.

He issued a sharp sigh.

"Then what choice do I have?" he asked with a shrug.

"Good," she said. "We have an agreement. The lawyer will be in shortly."

Quint nodded to the guard who'd been standing at the window with his arms crossed. He unfolded his arms and retrieved Vadik. It had been a long but productive day. Everything was sore and Ree was exhausted. Time to head back to the apartment.

As soon as they stepped into the hallway and the door was closed, Quint brought Ree into an embrace.

"We need to get you home and to bed," he said, then caught the implication. "Not for that. Although I'm ready and willing the second you feel up to it."

He winked and it made her smile. His smile brought to life places that needed rest.

She pushed up to her tiptoes and pressed a kiss to his lips. She'd been wanting to do that all day.

"You'll be the first to know when I'm able," she said, then wiggled her eyebrows. "Are you ready to get out of here?"

"There's no place like home," he quipped, linking their fingers as they headed out toward the same way they had come. The desk sergeant came and unlocked the door for them before thanking them for coming by.

The ride home was short. Ree ate a ham sandwich before rinsing off in another shower. It would take a month of showers to wash off the creepy feeling of being buried alive. She threw on pajamas and hit the bed.

"I'll join you after a shower," Quint said, kissing her good-night.

She could get used to this. In fact, she *would* get used to it once this case was over and they planned their wedding. As it was now, Quint was trying to infiltrate a higher level in A-12 and get close enough to Dumitru to pin him for the crimes he committed. Was *still* committing. The arrest she prayed was coming would have to stick, so they needed to be very careful with how they went about collecting evidence. One slip could be used against them in court, allowing Dumitru to walk. Was the system flawed? Yes, she could honestly say it was.

Was it necessary to dot every *i* and cross every *t*? Absolutely yes. Did it mean some folks walked? The fact burned her up inside.

But Ree didn't want to churn over a system that needed tweaks. All she wanted to do was think about the progress they'd made and the fact that, at some point tomorrow, Vadik would be "dead."

Kicking the case into high gear meant closing it that much faster. It was an idea Ree could get behind. In her mind, she'd already started writing her letter of resignation for her boss, Lynn Bjorn.

QUINT WOKE BEFORE REE, slipped out from underneath the covers and logged on to the system to check the status of the case. Securing Vadik's help would move the case along. He hoped. Quint needed to provide a status update to Lindy since the man was still under the impression Quint was a bad guy. Surely he would know by now that Ree was no longer in the box. Should Quint let the man sweat it? Wonder where she could be?

While the system was booting up, he circled

around the counter into the kitchen and made coffee. His mind was still foggy, and he realized he hadn't checked his cell phone. He'd left it on the nightstand. Coffee came first.

The machine beeped less than three minutes after he loaded it with water and grounds. The smell alone started the wheels turning in his brain. He needed to come up with a plan on how to handle Lindy today. Giselle was a whole other story. Quint had to work hard to control his anger. Of course, any normal person in a relationship would be raging mad at this point, and rightfully so. This was an opportunity to show loyalty to Lindy. As much as it galled Quint, he would do it.

Conjuring up the image of Tessa lying in the hospital bed was normally enough to bring insta-rage boiling in his veins. Either Ree was softening him, or maybe it was the idea of picking up his life and starting a family, but he wanted peace. Peace for Tessa. Peace for her child. And peace for him.

None of what he was currently doing would bring her or the baby back. In fact, she'd most likely chew him out for sticking with a case this long. He knew the risks. He wanted justice for his former best friend and what would have been his godchild. But he was beginning to want to build his own life even more.

If any of his actions could change the past, he had no problem continuing on this course. He'd seen it this far. Leaving now would cast suspicion. It would be impossible to insert another pair of agents into the case at this point. All momentum would be lost, and it could take another two or three years to get this close to Dumitru. The situation was too hot to introduce new players if Quint and Ree walked out. Like it or not, he was stuck with this one. And, like it or not, he needed to see it through to the end.

Would Tessa kick his ever-loving backside over going in this deep and half the stuff he'd pulled to get this far? Quint smirked. He knew the answer was a resounding *hell yeah*. It was getting easier to set some of his anger at the situation aside and see reason. Was Ree the difference in this new ability?

Again, the answer was yes. Being with her made him want to strive to become a better person. He wanted to deal with the emotional baggage he'd convinced a counselor he didn't have. There was something about Ree that made her see right through him to his core. She saw the real him, flaws and all, and seemed to love him anyway.

So, yeah, he wanted to give her everything she deserved in return. Did that mean dealing with his demons so he could move away from a haunted past and have children? Yes. Did that mean reconciling the past with Tessa? Yes.

If only Ree could have met his mother, and his best friend. Life could strip away loved ones at any moment, he realized. All he truly had was the here and now. He'd been reminded yesterday morning just how quickly someone could be stripped from his life forever.

The way folks drove in downtown Dallas, the possibility of being struck and killed by a vehicle wasn't all that far-fetched. Life was at best unpredictable and at worse cruel. And then someone like Ree had walked into his world, making him rethink everything he thought he knew about goodness and love. She was everything that was right in the world.

Movement in the adjacent bedroom meant she was waking up. He poured a second cup of coffee and brought in to her. Silky red hair splayed across the cream-colored pillowcase. She yawned and stretched her arms out before rolling over to where he sat.

"Well, hello there," she said, her sleepy voice tugging at his heartstrings. He was still trying to figure out how she'd ended up falling for a guy like him. He'd been rough around the edges when they'd met on the first case, but she'd seen something in him. The times they'd kissed had made him realize a spark had been missing from every one of the kisses he'd shared in the past.

Ree Sheppard had turned his world upside down. And he was all the better for it. She was like an angel descended from the heavens, made just for him, perfect in every way imaginable.

"Is that coffee?" she asked as he sat there, dumbstruck.

"For you." He handed over a cup as she sat up. The covers slid down to her waist, revealing the white cotton T-shirt that clung to her curves and revealed firm, full breasts pressed against the thin material.

Ree might be beautiful and have a body made for sinning, but it was her intelligence and sharp wit that had attracted him in the first place. She was the real deal of brains and beauty. Her sense of humor was right up there with his own on the rare occasion he saw it. And there had always been something about Ree that defined her, made her stand out from every other woman Quint had dated. The connection they shared was deeper and more electric than anything he'd ever known. Quint was still trying to figure out what he'd done to deserve her.

"Why so serious?" Ree asked. "Did something happen in the case?"

"No," he quickly said, not wanting her to worry before she had her first cup of coffee. "Nothing like that."

"Then what?" she asked.

He leaned forward and pressed a kiss to her full pink lips.

"I'm a lucky bastard," he said. "That's all."

Her smile could melt ice in a freezer with the door closed.

"I consider myself pretty lucky to have found you, Mr. Casey," Ree said, then took a sip of her coffee. Her tongue slicked across her lips, leaving a silky trail. It was a trail he was having a difficult time taking his eyes off of.

"How are you really feeling this morning?" he asked, needing to redirect his thoughts, because all he wanted to do was make love to his fiancée.

"Well enough to work," she said. "But not before brushing my teeth."

Quint set his cup of coffee on the nightstand as Ree disappeared into the bathroom. She returned a few moments later after the whir of her electric toothbrush did its job. She immediately took a sip of coffee before straddling him on the bed. He splayed his hand on the small of her back, holding her in place so she didn't have to balance her weight. He brought his other hand up to her face, cupping her cheek and bringing her mouth down on his.

And then he made love to the woman he could hardly wait to start his life with. Because everything up to now seemed like a warm-up to the real deal.

"NOW THAT'S THE proper way to start a day," Ree teased as she gasped for air. Having had one of the best orgasms of her life, she figured this was just the beginning. They'd made love a few times on the assignment but not nearly enough, considering her fiancé had the hottest bod on the planet. She wanted to memorize every inch of him, every scar, every imperfection. Although there were very few of those on a man like Quint Casey and he was one of the rare few who made battered and bruised still look sexy.

"Agreed," he said in between deep breaths. "We need a vacation."

"I'd like a permanent one," she said with another smile. Work waited, and they couldn't stay in this position for long. For the moment, there was no other place she'd rather be than here with her head resting on his arm as it wrapped around her.

Quint's cell buzzed. He reached over to the nightstand and picked it up before checking the screen. "It looks like it's all been arranged and will go down at their breakfast this morning."

"Do we know what time breakfast is at the prison?" Ree asked, figuring their brief oasis of sanity was over.

"In about half an hour," Quint supplied.

"I guess we wait around until we get word it happened," she said. There was no way either of them could relax until it was done, so she threw off the sheets and got ready for the day.

After freshening up in the bathroom, she moved to the kitchen and refilled their coffee mugs. She checked the fridge to see what she could throw together to eat as Quint studied the laptop screen, no doubt reading up on all the case notes and updating the file. A lot had happened in the past twenty-four hours.

Ree pulled out a carton of eggs, a quart of milk and some leftover spinach from salads they'd had. She could throw together some decent scrambled eggs with the shredded cheese she found. No one would accuse her of being a good cook, but she knew enough to feed herself on the most basic level. There was a loaf of bread, so she could make toast. No jelly, but she could always make do with a dab of butter.

A knock at the door startled them both. Her gaze flew to Quint, who immediately jumped into action. A few seconds later, he was at the door with his weapon at the ready. He peeped through the hole in the door.

"Open up, Quint," a familiar female voice pleaded. What did Giselle think she was doing here?

Chapter Seven

Anger raged inside Ree. So much so, she didn't trust herself not to jump Giselle the second Quint opened the door.

"Why should I after what you pulled?" Quint asked as Ree scurried around, securing the laptop and cell phone after taking his weapon. She pointed toward the wall of closets in the bedroom.

"Is she here?" Giselle asked.

"I think we both know you don't care what happens to my partner," he said, disdain dripping from his tone. Ree figured he didn't have to do a whole lot of acting to pull it off. She felt her own anger in a place deep in her bones. Betrayal could do that to a person.

With all the accessories in hand, she climbed into the closet in the adjacent bedroom and shut the door. Giselle needed to wonder a little while longer what happened to Ree. Her hands pressed against the wood as she crouched inside the small dark space. Memories of being surrounded by nothing but wood flooded her, and she had to remind herself to breathe as her chest squeezed. This wasn't yesterday morning. Ree could open the door at any time and be free. She repeated those thoughts until she started to believe them, and her pulse slowed down a few notches below panic.

"I'll open the door, but if there is someone waiting out of view, Giselle, I promise you that I will hunt you down," Quint threatened.

"There isn't, and I'm taking a huge risk coming here. Open the door and hear me out," Giselle begged. "At the very least, get me out of this hall-way."

Thankfully, their undercover apartment was small and open enough for Ree to be able to hear everything that was going on in the next room from the closet. She took note since she didn't exactly want her neighbors to know every time she and Quint were intimate. Then again, she hadn't heard noise from other apartments since they'd started living there. It was highly possible the walls in between places were thicker. The door would leak noise since it wasn't exactly made of hardwood. This place had a high-end look, but the contractors had cheated in spots with the materials, making it easy to hear everything inside the open-concept space.

It dawned on Ree what her next career move might be. She shelved the thought for now, but she'd always noticed the small details in a house or apartment or how she might do things differently.

"You have a helluva lot of explaining to do." Quint's voice practically boomed as she heard the door open and then close. Then came the snick of the lock.

"Is she here?" Giselle repeated, her voice sounded near frantic at this point. Still, it was impossible to forgive the woman.

"Does it look like it? Look around." Quint's voice sounded wild with worry and steeped in anger. Was this how he'd felt yesterday afternoon, realizing she was gone? Ree's heart pounded against her rib cage as she thought about what might have gone wrong and how terrible it must have been for Quint to sit on the sidelines, not knowing where she was or what she was doing. Or what might have happened to her. His mind had to have flashed back to Tessa. Did that explain his sudden change of heart on the possibility of children?

"You need to start talking and tell me where she is," he demanded.

"I—I—I don't even know where to start." From the way Giselle's voice came in and out of clarity, Ree guessed the woman was pacing. She should be very nervous being around Quint after the stunt she'd pulled. Not to mention the fact Ree and Quint had access to Axel, her boyfriend and her baby's father, who was currently in prison. He'd been the one who struck a deal for his family's safety in exchange for Giselle getting Ree and Quint in with Vadik. Once this case was resolved, Giselle and her young son would be offered Witness Protection, unbeknownst to her. Axel had arranged everything. He'd said she would agree to WITSEC after he spoke to her, which couldn't happen until Dumitru was behind bars.

"Then why are you here?" Quint's voice was the equivalent of thunder booming. It practically shook the walls when he spoke.

"Because I need you both to know I had nothing to do with what happened," Giselle said. "It wasn't my idea, and I fought hard against Lindy. With Vadik in jail right now, Lindy is having a field day."

"I know you were involved. I just don't know what you did," he said. "But she would have let her guard down because she trusted you."

The disdain in his voice permeated the space.

"I didn't have a choice. Lindy said I had to lure her out of the apartment, or he'd take little Axel away, and I'd never see my boy again. What would Axel think of me if I lost our child?" she said, her voice a mix of scared and whiny. Ree liked neither. She could, however, sympathize with a mother who was doing what she could to protect her son.

The truth was that Giselle seemed to like hanging out at Vadik's penthouse more than being home or a mother to her son—a son, she had to remind herself, who currently lived with Giselle's sister. What kind of a mother shoved her kid off to the side and then partied all the time? Not a good one. It also had Ree thinking she needed to cut her own mother a little more slack. Not that she was ready to forgive and move on, but at the very least, Ree's mother cared about her daughter's safety. The fact her mother was too judgmental about Ree's personal choices didn't diminish the fact Ree had always known she was loved. Her older brother Shane would be the first one to point it out. He was their mother's favorite, so he would know.

Ree also noted Lindy liked to hit people directly in their hearts by threatening their families or those they loved. He'd kidnapped Ree to force Quint's hand into arranging a prison murder.

"Did you ever think of what might happen to Ree?" Quint pressed.

"Of course I did. I begged Lindy not...not to..." She seemed too choked up to go on.

"Not to what?" Quint insisted.

"Put her in that coffin, bury her and leave here there to force your hand," Giselle said, pleading her own case. She was all about self-survival, and yet those statements were actually true. She had gone to bat for Ree and sounded remorseful about the situation.

Ree was going to have to find a way to let it go and move on. They'd made a deal with Axel to protect Giselle and then offer WITSEC for her and their son. Ree would have to honor that commitment no matter how much she wanted to throttle the woman.

"My girlfriend might be out there lying in a ditch somewhere," he fired back. "You're taking me to the spot where you left her."

"I already went there," Giselle stated with more of that sorrow in her voice. She did seem genuinely upset about the whole situation. She'd been in survival mode and would be for the rest of her life if she always stayed tangled up in a relationship with criminals. "She's gone. The box is open."

"Box?" Quint had to pretend he didn't already know what had happened. His years of undercover work made it impossible to detect he was lying, and yet Ree would know if she looked in his eyes. They had a special bond, a connection like she'd never felt before in a relationship.

"Lindy did it. He forced her into a coffin to scare her and keep her from fighting," Giselle explained. It was halfway true. But then, could Ree really expect someone like Giselle to come completely clean?

"And then what?" More of that thunder rumbled in his voice.

"He started shoveling dirt on top of her," Giselle said in a helpless tone. "I stopped him, though. I put my foot down and got him to listen to me. I convinced him to walk away and go back to get her today. But he's going to flip out when he realizes she isn't there."

"And what exactly does that mean to you?" Quint asked.

Now they were getting to the real truth of why Giselle had shown today since she'd known it wasn't purely out of concern for Ree.

"He'll take away my baby, Quint. My son will never be safe again. Lindy is already suspicious of me, but then, he's paranoid of everyone," she continued. The voice stopped moving, which meant she'd planted her feet. It took all of Ree's willpower not to come out of that closet, because she had a sneaky suspicion Giselle was about to hit on Ree's man.

"There's nothing I can do about that," Quint said. Based on the volume of his voice, he'd moved into the kitchen. Was he putting a barrier between him and Giselle?

Ree's muscles coiled as she hunkered down. It seemed like a good time to remind herself this was a case. Giselle's actions weren't anything personal. Besides, how could anyone be trusted who hit on the first person she saw? Okay, the statement wasn't exactly true. Giselle seemed picky about who she spent time with, but hitting on Quint was her in pure survival mode. It must be awful to be at everyone else's mercy. Ree couldn't understand people like Giselle. Wasn't it so much harder to worry about where her next meal was going to come from or who she had to please over getting a job and taking care of herself and her son?

Granted, she might have to give up the penthouse party life, but what was that giving her? Status?

To Ree's thinking, status didn't put food on the table every night for a kid. It would do Giselle a world of good to kick off those stilettos and put on a pair of sneakers. Plenty of people were hiring. The woman might have to start at the bottom, but she could build a life from there. It would be honest work that Giselle could feel good about at the end of the day. Ree thought of Zoey, a young woman from a previous case who Ree had helped get into an abused women's shelter in Austin after the that case came to a close.

Zoey had adopted a dog and was working. She had plans for the future. The changes in her since getting the help she needed were astounding. Ree had so much respect for Zoey. All she'd needed was a little push in the right direction. Now she was thriving and building a life from the ground up.

Did Giselle think she was too good to start at the bottom? Because Ree had news for the woman: she wasn't doing very well on the party circuit. Give it a couple more years and she would age out. Or worse, end up working for the crime ring. She would be pulled deeper into a life that would chew her up and spit her out. But that was her choice to make.

"Please help me," Giselle begged.

"Take a couple of steps away from me and toward the door or I'll pick you up and throw you out myself," Quint practically growled.

"Sorry," Giselle said. "Don't you think I'm pretty enough?"

"Not the point," he quipped.

"I know that I'm not her, but she might never come back again, Quint. You have to face facts, and we could be a powerful team," Giselle said

Ree's blood boiled at hearing those words, and it was taking everything inside her not to remove herself from that closet immediately.

QUINT SHOULDN'T HAVE been surprised at the offer from Giselle. And yet there he was, dumbfounded by the fact she thought it was acceptable to walk right into the home he shared with Ree and hit on him.

"Out," was all he said, all he could say without losing it. He'd gotten everything from this conversation he wanted to know. And now she needed to go before Ree climbed out of that closet and dragged Giselle out of the apartment in a body bag.

Giselle didn't put up much of a fight. She seemed to know when she'd lost a battle. Quint figured Ree had even more reasons to throat-punch her betrayer after this visit. Quint shook his head as he heard the elevator ding, and then the doors open and close, but he checked the peephole anyway just to be certain Giselle was gone.

The second Ree must've heard the front door close, she sprang from the closet. She also must have remembered how easily sound echoed from the hallway, because she held her tongue even though it was easy to see from the tension lines on her face she had a lot on her mind.

He shot her a look that he hoped would help calm her down, then checked the peephole again to be one hundred percent certain Giselle had left the floor.

"She's gone," he said to Ree before walking over and pulling her into his arms. She buried her face in his chest.

"I don't know what it is about the sound of her voice that had me wanting to climb out of my skin. I must still be associating her with that box," Ree said. "It took all my willpower not to strangle her."

"No one would blame you if you had," Quint reassured her, holding her as she trembled. The experience from yesterday must have impacted her a whole lot more than he realized, because she was the strongest person he knew.

"And then she hit on you," Ree stated.

"The move reeks of desperation," he explained.

"She is clearly good at saving her own hide," Ree continued. "Although, I must say, she wasn't lying when she said that she convinced Lindy not to bury the box. She will probably go down for my escape because of it."

"You could have suffocated otherwise," Quint said. "That couldn't have been what he wanted. He had to know I would come after him like a pit bull locked onto a side of beef."

"She fought hard for me. I heard it. And he could be just that arrogant," Ree pointed out.

"True. It's like the frog in the pot when the temperature is only turned up one degree at a time. The frog doesn't even feel it until it's too late," he agreed. In truth, it was the same with most criminals. They got away with something small before moving on to bigger crimes, better takes. Over time, their confidence grew. Many ended up getting cocky and thinking they were untouchable. That was when mistakes happened. Without those mistakes, the smartest criminals would end up doing a whole lot more damage. On the side of the law, strict rules had to be followed so no one's rights were violated during the evidence gathering process. While Quint cursed having to go about things the right way from time to time, he realized how important it was to follow protocol.

As far as those who were guilty as sin, they never got away with it for long on Quint's watch.

"It's going to be my pleasure to slap cuffs on Lindy, lock him up, and throw away the key," Ree said, and the fierceness in her eyes showed she meant every word.

An uneasy feeling settled over Quint. Cases took time to develop. They just didn't have it to give, and he had no idea when the sand was going to run through the hourglass.

Chapter Eight

It has gone down.

The text indicating Vadik's fake murder came an hour after breakfast. Quint set his phone on the counter and locked gazes with Ree. He took in a deep breath with the full knowledge the bubble they'd been in this morning was about to burst. The real world and the case were about to take over their lives until arrests were made. The few hours of quiet they'd shared had to be enough to hold them over.

Quint had an "in" with Lindy now. Another adventure was about to begin.

"What do we know about Lindy?" he asked, figuring he needed to be briefed as much as possible before heading over to Lindy's place. The penthouse where Vadik used to live would be off limits now.

"Rolph Lindberg has been Dumitru's right-hand man for the past two and a half years," Ree supplied as she hunkered over the laptop, studying the screen. "There isn't a whole lot known about him other than he kind of appeared on the scene and was directly tied to Dumitru. Lindy is from the same village in Romania as Dumitru, and the two are believed to have known each other long before they came to America."

"I'm guessing Lindy hasn't been fingerprinted, and there's no information about him in the Integrated Automated Fingerprint Identification System IAFIS database," Quint said.

"You would be right. There's no birth record that can be traced to his name, so it could be an alias," Ree stated. "I wouldn't be surprised one bit if that was the case, actually."

"A new identity for a new country," Quint said. It was an old trick and how the same criminals were able to go back and forth easily. A new identity, a new passport was only a forgery away.

"Other countries also don't keep the same kinds of records we're used to. You already know that," Ree stated.

"So, basically, this guy was a ghost until he came here to work for Dumitru, right?" Quint asked.

"Yes," she responded. "So there isn't much else to say except that he lives four blocks over from Vadik in an even nicer building."

"Are you thinking what I am?" Quint immediately asked.

"Dumitru has to live around here somewhere," she confirmed. It was the only thing that made sense if two of his closest advisors lived locally.

"How have we not seen him yet?" Quint asked.

"We've only been downtown a few weeks," Ree

pointed out. "Also, I highly doubt he visits Lindy or visited Vadik." She snapped her fingers a few times. "It might not hurt for me to change my appearance and follow Lindy around for a few days."

"We can get someone else to do that," Quint offered.

Ree shot him a look that made him realize he needed to address his statement.

"Hear me out," he started. "Lindy knows what you look like. It's the only reason for the suggestion. Even with a hair change or dye, you're distinct."

Ree sat there, quietly contemplating what he said. She always sat back in her chair and rounded her shoulders forward a little when she was concentrating. Another telltale sign was the concern line creasing her forehead. It also showed up when she was studying something carefully like the laptop screen or her phone. Speaking of which, they needed to get her a new cell phone.

A man with a ghost of a past wasn't exactly someone Quint liked to go after. They were too slippery.

"Fair point on not being able to change my look so drastically that I could be absolutely certain Lindy wouldn't recognize me," Ree stated.

"I'll contact Bjorn and request more resources on the case," he said.

"Are you sure this has nothing to do with what happened yesterday morning?" Ree asked.

"I'd be lying if I said I wasn't bothered at my very core over what happened," he admitted. All he could do was be one hundred percent honest with her. "Believe me when I say there's no other agent I'd rather be working with on the professional side. On the personal side, I'm a work in progress."

"I'm capable," she began.

"I know," he said. "It's the reason I don't want to work with anyone else. But I can't ignore my personal feelings for you either. Can you honestly say that being in love hasn't changed the way you feel about me going out to do my job?"

"It has," she stated. "This whole relationship caught me off guard, and it's all new territory. I respect what you do, and I know you're the best. But there's this piece of me that remembers the look in my mother's eyes after my dad stopped coming home. The way she left his clothes in his closet for years like he was going to walk through the door any second and reclaim them. In fact, I didn't even want to acknowledge these emotions were still there until we started talking about it just now. Is that weird?"

"Not to me, it isn't," he said.

"I'll bring up a map of the city, and we can see if Grappell can get a floor plan for Lindy's building, as well," Ree said, changing the subject before he could say anything else. It was probably the stress of the case that had her thoughts all over the place.

He walked over to her and planted a tender kiss on her lips.

"Are we okay?" he asked, feeling like she'd just shut down and shut him out.

"Of course," she said, kissing him back despite the fact there was no conviction in those words.

"Good." This didn't seem like the appropriate time to dig into why a wall seemed to have just come up between them. Their personal life needed to be put on hold a little while longer until he could finish what he'd started with the case. They were close. He could feel it.

Lindy would be the ticket in to Dumitru. Everything else could be dealt with when this case was behind them.

Quint picked up his cell phone and sent a text to Lindy confirming the murder had taken place.

Proof?

Quint issued a sharp sigh. Then he fired off a text to Grappell, who immediately sent a picture of a bloodied Vadik. His gaze was fixed and his skin pale. Quint forwarded the pic, and then asked, Where is my wife?

The response came quickly.

Complication. Meet me. Lindy gave an address that Quint recognized as Lindy's building.

"He wants to meet," Quint said to Ree.

"That's good," she said a little too quickly. She put on a smile he instantly recognized as forced. Instinct said he should stop what he was doing and make her a priority. He should stop right there and ask her what was really wrong and, better yet, what he could do to make it better. They'd covered a lot of topics lately, and emotions had been running high since her kidnapping yesterday.

Quint needed to clear his head before he tackled

more serious subjects with Ree. The only way to do that was to put all this behind them.

"Looks like he wants me to come to him," he said, staring at his screen instead of watching her try to hide her disappointment.

"Be careful," she warned. "He has a few tricks up his sleeve."

Quint didn't respond with anything other than another kiss. He didn't know what to say to make things better between them. "I'll be back as soon as I can."

"Text me," she said, and then it seemed to dawn on her that she'd lost her phone.

He walked over to the closet where he kept the locked tackle box. He produced a key and then opened the lid. The lock kept their personal identities secure in the event prying eyes found it. There was a backup cell phone inside. He pulled it out for her.

"Here you go," he said after locking, then replacing the box. He held a new phone on the flat of his palm.

He probably should have been concerned when she didn't look up at him. Instead, she took the cell and turned around to face the laptop screen.

"How do you plan to go inside? Hot or cool?" she asked, and he knew exactly what she was talking about.

"Hot," he admitted. Any person worth their salt in a relationship would be blindly angry over what had happened to Ree. "I can buy a couple of days for you. Tell him that you called from a gas station today after walking all night. I'll say you're so angry at me for allowing this to happen that I don't know when you'll be back."

"Sounds good," she said without argument, and the knot in his gut tightened.

"I'll text when I can," he offered.

"Okay," she said. "Quint, don't let them trick you like they did me."

"I'll see what I can do." He touched her hand before securing a gun in his ankle holster and then walking out the door. At least she could lay low for a few days and catch her breath while he did some of the heavy lifting on the case. Besides, he was getting closer to Dumitru. Quint could feel it. And what needed to happen was between the two of them.

Quint scanned the street as he exited their building. It was midmorning by this point, closer to lunch than breakfast. With every step closer to Lindy, Quint's mood intensified. The non-fight he'd had with Ree had set him on edge. How was he supposed to know what to do with their relationship? He didn't exactly have all the answers. All he knew was that she was the one. He loved her more than anything in this world. The rest would work itself out. It had to. He couldn't imagine a life without her now that he'd found her.

She'd brought up her mother and the fact her father had been killed on the job in law enforcement. Was she getting cold feet in their relationship? Figuring history was repeating itself?

Hell if he knew what was on her mind. She didn't seem to have it all figured out either, which didn't help.

Quint had to push those thoughts aside as best he could to get his mind in the right space for the meetup with Lindy. This was exactly the reason it was a bad idea to mix personal with business. Falling in love was a distraction. Being overly protective was a distraction. Thinking about a future and kids was a distraction.

Quint hit the crosswalk to the sound of a horn blaring. He sidestepped the sedan that almost rammed him in the leg. He muttered a curse as he brought his hand up to wave. The driver flipped him off. Great.

For the rest of the walk, Quint kept his eyes on the road. When this case was over, he would have time to sit down and talk to her about how he felt. Right now, his one hundred percent focus needed to stay on getting to Dumitru.

Walking into the lobby of Lindy's building, Quint noticed the nothingness of the expansive space. The floors were some kind of fancy white marble tile. They were shiny, like walking on glass. A pair of flat wooden benches sat across from each other and on opposite sides of a white fur rug. Other than a few plants placed here and there, and a fireplace, there wasn't much else to the lobby. It gave minimalism a whole new meaning.

There were two men wearing almost all black standing near the elevator bank to the right. Quint didn't recognize them but would bet money they were connected to Lindy. Almost as soon as Quint had the thought, Lindy came around the corner. He flicked his gaze over to Quint before motioning toward the elevators with a nod.

Summoning all the frustration over the case and anger at this man kidnapping Ree to force Quint's hand, he made his way toward Lindy. The guy was all thick bushy eyebrows and facial hair. His dark eyes practically glared at Quint. He'd be damned if he let Lindy get away with pushing Ree around.

"You should have just come after me instead," Quint said as he charged into the two younger Romanians. They closed ranks. One of the men tried to push Quint back a couple of steps. His attempt was unsuccessful. Quint threw a shoulder into the man on his right and the guy backed to regain his balance.

Lindy's gaze widened. Did he seriously think Quint was going to lie down and allow a creep like this to walk all over him? It would strip any street cred he'd built throughout the case and basically invite others to treat him the same. It couldn't be allowed.

Guy number two reached behind his back. Quint knew exactly what was about to happen, and he didn't want this to escalate while it was still three against one.

He threw his hands in the air.

"All right," he said. "I'm good. There's no reason to whip out a gun."

The guy froze, keeping his hand back as though he might change his mind at any moment. He glanced over at Lindy, who gave a slight nod.

Quint wasn't finished with Lindy, but this wasn't the time or place to exact revenge. He reminded himself it wouldn't be too much longer, though.

"If you can control yourself," Lindy started, looking more shaken than he probably wanted to, "we can go upstairs now."

"Fine by me," Quint stated. "But let me know if you need to be reminded the wives and girlfriends stay out of this. Whatever happens is between you and me, and I expect it to stay that way. *Comprende?* Or should I turn around and walk right back out of the front door?"

Lindy offered what seemed like a reluctant nod.

"If anything had happened to her because of you, I would hunt you down and personally slit your throat. Do you understand?" Quint ground out as the elevator doors closed behind them. There were rules about respect and family that were followed even with the criminal element. In fact, those rules were etched in stone, and a person's family was off limits even if a relationship hadn't been made official by marriage.

Quint's hands fisted at his sides as he stared at Lindy.

"My mistake," Lindy acquiesced. His words sure sounded good, but Quint doubted the man would pull back even after the confrontation.

Lindy lived on the ninth floor of a twelve-story building. There were six apartments on his floor. Quint was surprised Lindy's apartment wasn't as expensive or flashy as Vadik's. Lindy's easily looked like a family might live here.

In fact, the door to the kitchen was closed, and Quint was certain he heard a female in there humming. Was Lindy a family man? He was a far cry from the bachelor Vadik.

The decor was the complete opposite of the lobby's. The sofa was a leather sectional that looked expensive but also gently worn. It faced a flat-screen that took up almost half the wall. The corner fireplace anchored the room. Paintings on the wall were from the Renaissance era, expensive and possibly original. This place reeked of old money and, Quint had to admit, good taste.

"Step outside?" Quint asked Lindy, motioning toward the balcony that was bricked halfway up. The structure looked solid.

Lindy's thugs started to go with them.

"Alone," Quint said.

With a look of reluctance, Lindy finally waved off his buddies.

Quint led the way outside, walked straight to the edge and listened for the sliding glass door to close. The second it did, he whirled around on Lindy, grabbing him by the throat before spinning him around. Quint walked Lindy until his back was against the bricks. He was bent over in a backbend.

One hand on the man's throat and the other on his jaw, Quint dug his fingers into meaty flesh. He heard the door open behind him.

"Take one more step and he goes over," Quint said without looking back. It was the first evening this month he could tell a break in the relentless Texas heat wasn't far away. He locked gazes with Lindy. "Tell them!"

Lindy made a couple of grunting noises as he tried to speak while Quint's hand was clamped around his throat. Quint eased his grip enough for the man to get out one word.

"Stop!" Lindy coughed. His eyes looked like they might bulge out of their sockets. A vein in his neck pulsed and throbbed. He had a face hardened by a life of crime, but none of that showed through right now.

"Babe?" a female voice said from much closer than Quint expected. "Everything okay out here?"

Chapter Nine

Lindy's gaze pleaded with Quint, who wasn't ready to budge. He had half a mind to throw the sonofabitch over the brick half wall right in front of the woman Quint assumed was Lindy's wife.

"C'mon," Lindy managed to say despite Quint tightening his grip. It would be so easy to cross the line right now and eradicate this filth from the earth forever. Blood rushed to Lindy's head, causing his face to turn beet red.

For more than a few seconds, Quint contemplated doing just that—ending this jerk's crime spree. But then he was reminded of the oath he'd taken to serve and protect. He recalled the real reason he was here in the first place. Tessa's face came to mind, and so did Ree's. He couldn't bring his best friend back, and he couldn't risk losing the only woman he'd ever truly loved by going to jail himself. Squeezing the life out of Lindy might feel good in the moment, but Quint didn't want to live with any more regret. And he would have remorse. First, for taking a life. Second, for ruining the investigation. Third, and most important, for losing Ree.

With a sharp sigh, Quint grabbed a fistful of Lindy's shirt and yanked him upright. He shot the man a murderous look.

"Go back in the kitchen," Lindy said through heaves. "Everything is fine out here. Just a misunderstanding."

Quint had had to make sure Lindy knew he wasn't the only one who could strike at what was important. Lindy's home should be sacred and respected. Since Lindy crossed a boundary with Quint, Quint was forced to reciprocate or appear weak. Being weak in a crew like this meant certain death.

"I did what you asked. Vadik is dead," Quint said, not budging an inch, standing toe-to-toe with Lindy. "Now, back off."

Lindy put his hands up, palms out, in the surrender position, but the sneer remained on his face. He didn't like being shown up in his own home and in front of his wife. There were probably kids inside somewhere too.

"You did everything I asked," Lindy said. "There's no reason to fight amongst ourselves. My orders came from someone else anyway."

Quint highly doubted Lindy would be ordered to kidnap Ree, but this wasn't the time to argue the point.

"You doubted Vadik's loyalty," Quint stated. "What's to say you won't turn on me?"

Lindy's sneer grew wider.

"It goes both ways," he said.

"Yes, it does. Try to remember that," Quint stated with more than a hint of threat in his voice. "Tread carefully, Lindy. If we're going to work together, you're going to have to find a way to trust me and not put my back against the wall."

"Point taken," Lindy said, his dark eyes boring holes through Quint.

"Where is she?" Quint demanded.

"I'm not allowed to give you that information," Lindy stated. "This meeting is over."

"That's where you're wrong. We haven't even begun," Quint practically growled.

"Walk out now or you'll never work for Dumitru," Lindy threatened.

"Who were you taking orders from?" Quint pressed. "I want to see him."

"You'll get your chance," Lindy stated. His gaze fixed on someone or something behind them.

The temptation to turn around and see who or what was back there was too great to pass up. Quint craned his neck around in time to see the backside of a male figure as he walked out the door into the hallway. The creepy-crawly feeling people referred to as a cat walking over their grave struck as the guy turned his head to the side and Quint got a glimpse of his profile. Dumitru?

From this distance and at a glance, it was impossible to be certain. Quint had to fight every instinct inside of him that wanted to bolt after the person who could be Dumitru and confront him. Keeping his cool, he reminded himself that he was here for the long game, the arrest, the evidence that would lock this man away for the rest of his life so he couldn't hurt anyone else.

"Was that your boss?" Quint turned his attention back to Lindy.

He was met with an eerie smile.

"Like I said, you'll find out soon enough," came Lindy's response. The man was a little too overconfident now. Quint didn't like the change in demeanor.

Taking a step back, he released his grip on Lindy.

"I'm all in with whatever you want or need me to do," Quint said. "But if you ever touch my woman again…"

Lindy swatted empty air.

"You already said," he responded. "The same goes for you if you ever walk into my house and pull anything like this."

"Turnabout is fair play," Quint stated.

"We're done here," Lindy ground out.

"You know how to reach me," Quint said before turning around and walking out the door. He half expected a bullet in his back and was pleasantly surprised when none came. He'd stood his ground and gave Lindy something to chew on in the process. Quint laid down the law and showed that he wouldn't be pushed around. Since the move hadn't killed him, he'd most likely earned a serious amount of street cred.

He missed the elevator Dumitru had disappeared onto by a solid couple of minutes. It had been necessary and, he hoped, his patience would bring him into the fold faster.

Quint didn't truly exhale until he was out in the fresh air. He wanted to check on Ree to see how she was doing or if she'd discovered anything while he was gone. She had probably dug into the case files, and he wanted her take on the information.

The walk home felt longer than it took. The closer he got to their building, an unsettled feeling took hold. He was up the elevator and back inside their apartment in a matter of minutes, but it sure felt like an hour. The way he'd left things earlier sat like hot lead in his gut.

Talking about their relationship and their future had to be put on hold. He only hoped Ree understood and could forgive him.

The minute he opened the door, she came around the corner to the foyer. Her gaze skimmed his body with urgency, and he realized she was looking for injuries or bullet holes.

"I'm okay. See?" He held his hands high in the air and performed a quick spin to accentuate the point.

Ree practically launched herself at him. He caught her and kissed her, hard and unyielding. Her lips were the equivalent of heaven on earth, and her body pressed to his was the way he wanted to stay for a solid week when this was all said and done. Breakfasts in bed. A wedding. A honeymoon. The works.

When she finally pulled away, she caught his gaze.

"How did it go?" she asked. "Tell me everything."

He linked their fingers and walked over to the couch before spilling all the details of what had gone down.

"Good move on your part," she said when he told her about his attack on Lindy.

"Anything less would have placed an even bigger target on my back," he said.

She nodded agreement. The tension lines in her forehead eased but not enough to go away.

"What did you learn?" she asked.

"I now know where Lindy lives and that he has a wife. I believe he has kids, but I didn't get a look at them. His place is the opposite of Vadik's in pretty much every sense. And he is successful. I saw paintings on the walls that probably belonged in museums and not some random person's home," he explained. Then added, "I'm almost certain Dumitru was there too."

Ree gasped.

"Why don't you know for certain?" she asked, and he could already tell what she was thinking. If she'd been there, she could have followed Dumitru.

"I only saw his profile from a distance, and there were others in my line of sight. Now, those folks wanted to take my head off," he said with a chuckle that failed miserably at lightening the mood.

"I've been doing a little research myself," she said with a glint in her eyes that said she found something useful.

REE HAD DUG into case files rather than go crazy while waiting for Quint. The worst part about working with the man she loved was how losing him would shatter her. The death of any partner would be tragic and traumatic. Losing someone she respected, worked with, and intended to spend the rest of her life with would destroy her world.

"Dumitru has ties to a woman by the name of Lizanne Vega," Ree informed him. "She owns a 'toys' and lingerie shop on Central Expressway and Arapaho."

"I know the area. It would be an easy place to stake out, considering there's always a lot of traffic and noise in the shops in the area," Quint stated.

"Of course, I want to barge right in and lean on her, but the bull in a china shop method probably isn't the best course of action," Ree admitted. "The worst thing about being undercover is not being able to use a badge and a gun. Makes it hard to push people into talking."

"We could always send in a colleague. See who Bjorn or Grappell recommends," Quint stated.

"Could make her nervous, and then she'd tell him not to come around," she reasoned.

"I did get the sense from Lindy and his guys that everyone in the organization is on edge right now," Quint said.

"The fact they want anyone who gets arrested to be erased almost instantly is another giveaway," she pointed out.

"Is there a romantic tie between Lizanne and Dumitru?" Quint asked.

"Let me show you her pictures." Ree retrieved

the laptop and pulled up a photo of the store. It had Lizanne pictured in sexy lingerie. "I'm guessing she supplies clothes to the local exotic dancers."

Dallas was well known for its topless bars.

"It's possible she has a few friends in the clubs, then," he said. "Or could be friends with the owners."

"I was surprised to find Dumitru linked to anyone in a business that could shed light on his operation. Topless clubs in Dallas are heavily monitored by local police as they do tend to attract a seedy element," Ree stated.

Quint pulled out his wallet and the crinkled piece of paper with the tree drawing on it. He'd been carrying it around so long the edges were tattered. He smoothed it out on the coffee table. Dumitru's name sat at the top with two long branches below. One was marked "Lindy." The other was marked "Vadik." Quint retrieved a pen and crossed off Vadik's name. He added a smaller branch and added Lizanne's name.

"We can always drop a surveillance camera in the parking lot. It's a public lot, so we wouldn't need to obtain permission first," Ree offered.

Quint nodded and smiled.

"We could drop a listening device in the shrubbery if there is any," he added.

Ree looked up the shop online, pulling up the location on Google Maps. "The name of her place isn't exactly creative."

She pointed to the name, Adult Lingerie, written in cursive. The sign on the strip mall center was in red.

"No one is going to mistake the place for a family pajama store," Quint mused with a chuckle.

"You got that right," she agreed, looking at the street view and seeing mannequins in the window that were wearing garter belts and fishnet stockings. She didn't even want to know if that was allowed or against code in a state that didn't allow alcohol sales before 10 a.m. on Sundays.

Ree gave a mental headshake.

"Ready to take a ride over?" she asked.

"You're not too tired?" he asked. It was getting late.

"I'll sleep better if I feel like I've accomplished something today," she admitted.

"Let's do this," came the response.

"I'll drive," she said, figuring he'd done enough for one night.

They filed down to the waiting SUV after locating a couple of devices to drop near Adult Lingerie. The Chevy was sitting in the exact spot where they'd left it. Ree walked the perimeter anyway, checking for bombs or tracking devices. When she deemed it safe, she gave the go-ahead to Quint, who had just finished walking his side.

She climbed in the driver's seat as Quint rummaged around in the back seat. He produced a pair of baseball caps.

"These are better than nothing," he stated, handing one over after placing the other on top of his head. Ree put hers on, lowering the bill as far as she could.

There wasn't a whole lot of traffic on 35E heading toward Central Expressway at this hour of the evening, so it didn't take long to reach Adult Lingerie. Ree drove past the strip shopping center, sticking to the service road and slowing down enough to get a good look at the area.

"Why would there be a light on in the back of the store at this late hour?" Ree asked as they drove past.

"You got me," he said. "Except there's a motorcycle parked on this side of the lot."

Part of the lot was obscured by shrubs that reached high enough to shroud vehicles parked close to the service road. Ree figured that was done on purpose to protect clients who didn't want to be caught parking in the lot. The other establishments were a CBD oil shop, a smoke shop and a deli.

And then it dawned on her.

"Didn't you say there was a motorcycle at the bust where Tessa…" Ree didn't finish the sentence, and she didn't need to.

"I sure as hell did," Quint responded. His gaze locked onto the parking lot as they passed.

"I'll swing back around. Give me a minute." She hit the gas and made a U underneath the highway, then another to get back on the proper side of the service road.

Since there were no cars on the road, she slowed to a crawl rather than go into the near-empty parking lot and possibly get unwanted attention.

"It's not the only vehicle in the lot," she said as she realized a small black sports car was parked alongside the motorcycle.

"It has been a while since the bust, and my mind could be playing tricks on me," Quint admitted. "I'm going to be real honest, though, and say that looks like Dumitru's bike."

Chapter Ten

Twice in one day.

Quint didn't want to push his luck, but the idea of being this close to Dumitru caused his danger radar to skyrocket.

"What do you want to do about it?" she asked. They couldn't legally track his movements without filing the proper paperwork first. He technically wasn't a suspect and hadn't been tied to a crime. There'd been no fingerprints of his on the scene, only a trail leading straight to the man. No one so far had been willing to testify against him, and the people who could seemed to turn up dead a little too regularly.

"Speed up." He slid down low in the seat as movement inside the shop caught his eye. "Did you see that?"

"No. What happened?" Ree asked.

"Someone is coming outside," he stated.

"I'll whip back around but can't promise I'll get back in time," she said. "Anything else and we'd be too obvious."

"A guy like Dumitru will be looking over his shoulder," Quint agreed. He just hoped she could make the circle fast enough to see which way he was going. This might just lead them to his home address. Since he didn't own anything in his name, there were no property records tied to him. In fact, Grappell had run Dumitru through the motor vehicle database and came up empty as well. It was a common trick for a career criminal not to have any property tied back to his or her own name. Except for Lizanne here.

"Does Lizanne have a record?" he asked, realizing he hadn't before.

"Nothing recent," Ree said. "She was brought up on charges of check fraud years ago, but it looks like she's been running a clean business for the past decade."

"He could be laundering money through her storefront," Quint said.

"We already know how easy it is for some of these store owners to have 'extra' merchandise in the backroom," she said.

Vadik had kept the kids he'd planned to traffic in his own store for safekeeping. It was easy considering shipments came in through the back. Large trucks parked as close to the rear door as they could get, making it difficult for anyone who happened to be nearby to see what was coming in and out. There were regulations that had to be followed, but it was easy to stay unseen in the back of a place like this one. Considering there was a smoke shop and a CBD oil shop, these weren't exactly neighbors who would be too nosy about what was going on in Lizanne's place other than to possibly ogle the customers as they came through.

There were a few vehicles zipping around on the highway. If the motorcycle rider hopped on Central Expressway, it would be a lot easier for Ree and Quint to follow without being too conspicuous.

"What do we have on Dumitru so far?" Ree asked. "Other than our suspicion he's the ringleader of A-12?"

"We have more than suspicion. There's Axel, for one. And Vadik," he said.

"Is that him?" she asked as the motorcycle pulled out of the parking lot and drove towards the on-ramp.

Ree followed far back enough they could keep watch but hopefully not far enough to lose him. To be fair, there was a smattering of vehicles on Central and no other motorcycles.

"Yes," Quint confirmed.

"What's he doing now?" Ree asked as the motorcycle exited on Belt Line Road. He'd been heading south and, Quint assumed, back home.

"I have no idea why this joker would get on the highway and then hop back off unless for evasive measures," Quint stated.

"Have you ever seen any of his top guys without security around?" she asked as she followed the motorcycle off the expressway.

"As a matter of fact, no, I haven't," he said. She was right. He'd never seen Vadik without an entourage. Maybe he was seeing what he wanted to with Dumitru instead of what was actually there. Plenty of folks rode motorcycles in the Dallas area. All the times Quint had been in the city for cases proved it to be true. He would never know why anyone would want to be on a motorcycle during rush hour, but he'd seen it.

"Hold on," she said as they both watched the man take the U-turn underneath the expressway. "Are you kidding me?"

"Drive a block or two up," Quint stated, but he had a hunch she already planned to do just that. "If we lose him, we lose him. It can't be helped." It might not even be Dumitru.

Ree issued a sigh, watching helplessly as the motorcycle disappeared from both of their views.

"It's hard to be this close and have to hold back," she said, stopping at the light. She smacked the flat of her palm against the steering wheel. "And now we'll really be behind the eight ball."

"I'd rather lose him tonight than be made because we got too anxious," he said.

"I would never jeopardize the case by being over-eager," she protested as the light finally changed and she hit the gas pedal.

"I know you wouldn't, and I'm normally the definition of patience," he said. "This case gets to me. Throws me off my game."

Ree didn't immediately respond. She drove to the next light and made the turnaround. The sound of a motorcycle gunning it and heading south on the highway in the direction she was heading gave Quint hope this night wasn't a total loss.

"He's just trying to throw anyone who might be following him off the trail. He literally must have made a circle and then hopped back on the expressway," he said.

"Oh, I don't know, Quint," she said. "How do you know it's not just a person on a motorcycle? That does happen on our wide-open roads, especially at night."

"Hop on the expressway in the direction we were originally headed and we'll see," he said.

"If we can catch him," she said as she took the next on-ramp. She floored the Chevy's gas pedal.

There was a decent dotting of cars out at half past midnight. This seemed to be the time folks really decided to go for it, racing by like the Chevy was a go-kart as it got up to speed with the flow.

"There's no way we're going to find him again," she said under her breath.

"His helmet was distinct. There was an orange glow-in-the-dark all-seeing eye on the back," Quint mentioned.

"That should give us a direction," she said.

Quint was just about to call it when he heard a noise up ahead. "Do you hear that?"

"I sure do," Ree stated, getting the Chevy up to speed as fast as it could go.

"It's him," Quint stated. The sticker was unmistakable.

Ree slowed enough to blend in behind a Dodge

Ram truck. "If we stay back here, we should be okay."

"He should be making the turnoff," Quint said. "He's about to pass the last exit for downtown."

"Is it possible he lives south of Dallas?" she asked.

"Anything is possible," he said, even though he'd pegged Dumitru for someone who would live close to Lindy and Vadik.

"He could be delivering something," Ree hedged. "Never mind. We both know he wouldn't be the one doing the dirty work."

"It's what will make him hard to pin down for any of his crimes," Quint agreed. In fact, he needed a more concrete plan to be able to nail him against the wall. The trail would be difficult. At this point, Quint's brain was running around in circles as to how to nail the bastard for the crimes he was committing and directing others to commit.

"Let's just see where this guy is headed, and once we get an address, we can run it through Grappell and see if he comes up with anything," Ree said.

The assumption the guy on the motorcycle would exit was a mistake. He kept going past downtown and stayed on Central Expressway until it turned onto 45.

"What are the odds it's him?" Ree asked.

Basically, they were heading toward Houston.

"No idea," he said. "But if you get tired of driving, we can switch places. There's no need to pull over. We can make it work."

"I'm wide awake," she said. "Although I wouldn't argue against a cup of coffee at this point."

"Looks like we're in this for the long haul to-night," he said. "As soon as it's feasible, we'll stop off and get a cup."

Ree glanced in the rearview as lights brightened behind them. "What's this jerk's problem?"

Someone had on their high beams, and it was annoying. Then it became dangerous as the larger vehicle roared up to the bumper. Quint pulled his weapon from his ankle holster and took aim.

IMPACT SNAPPED REE'S head forward. She muttered a string of curses as she gripped the wheel and swung right to avoid a second tap on her bumper as Quint climbed into the back seat. There were too few vehicles on the road to weave in and out of or provide any sort of protection, and her first thought was keeping innocent bystanders safe.

"Hang on back there," she warned as she cut a hard left. "I guess we weren't as sly as we thought we were."

"Clearly not," Quint stated. "I can't see anything clearly with those high beams on."

"Let me try to get beside him," Ree said. "Are you holding on?"

"Sure am," he confirmed.

Ree slammed on the brakes, grateful for the person who invented seat belts at this point. She was also thankful the tap to her bumper hadn't been hard enough to deploy airbags.

Was this person trying to scare her? Run her off the road? Let her know she and Quint had been seen following the motorcycle? There was no doubt in Ree's mind who the motorcycle belonged to now. And it seemed the turnaround earlier had been meant to shake them off Dumitru's tail. This guy was sophisticated and smart. Those two traits were the reason he sat on top of the organization and not in jail where he should be. Not yet, anyway.

The larger vehicle she assumed was a souped-up SUV mirrored her lane change. There were half a dozen cars dotting the highway on this stretch. The motorcycle had been baiting them. He was long gone. She should have realized he would put the pedal to the metal. He'd hung back to give his security detail a chance to catch up.

Ree mashed the brake. Hard. Quint's hand slammed against her seat as he braced himself. She cut the wheel right in time to miss being hit from behind.

"Sorry," she said.

"No worries," he shot back.

Since the motorcycle wasn't in sight, she figured exiting the highway would be the best course of action. Her training and skills with evasive maneuvers weren't doing much good on a long and flat stretch of highway with citizens on the road.

Ree banked right at the last minute, catching the exit ramp just in time. She glanced in her rearview, hoping she'd been able to shake their tail. No such luck. The SUV seemed to anticipate the move.

She was being too predictable.

The next on-ramp was tempting, considering there wasn't much else around. On the one hand, it was probably good that most citizens were in bed, fast asleep. In this case it worked against her. Open roads were the enemy of evasive tactics.

The SUV came close to nailing her back bumper but pulled away last minute. Why?

"What is going on?" Ree shouted. Adrenaline coursed through her, bringing all her senses to life. Blood thumped through her veins. Her heart pounded against her rib cage. These rushes were part of the job, a part she used to enjoy. Not so much any longer.

What had happened to her? How did she become the person her mother wanted her to be? A little voice in the back of her mind picked that moment to say she was getting older and was starting to want something different out of life. It didn't mean her mother had gotten into her head and changed her in any way.

"Watch out," Quint stated. "They're coming for us."

The answer to Ree's question about what was going on came when the SUV barreled up to the back of the driver's side and then made a hard right, smacking into her vehicle and sending her into a dangerous spin.

Within seconds, the Chevy flipped and started rolling down a ravine. It registered that Quint wasn't wearing a seat belt and should be flying all over the cab of the vehicle by now. Did he manage to secure himself somehow at the last minute?

The death roll of the Chevy seemed to slow time to a crawl. Her thoughts snapped to the fact they were out in the middle of nowhere, most likely near or on the outskirts of a cattle ranch with nothing and no one for miles except landscape. The ravine would make it impossible for anyone to see them from the highway.

Ree didn't know up from down by the time the Chevy stopped. Airbags had deployed. She felt every jolt and bang. The fact he was quiet sent a cold chill racing down her back.

Trying to get her bearings, she blinked a couple of times and reached for her seat belt.

"Quint?" she managed to get out against a suddenly dry throat. She swallowed in an attempt to ease some of the drought happening.

The fact he didn't respond sent more of those icy chills circulating through her. Worry seeded deep inside her. What if she lost the only man she'd ever truly loved?

As Ree's eyes began to focus and she started to get her bearings, she realized the Chevy was flipped on its side. Resolve started building within her. She needed to assess the situation and figure out how to get out of the vehicle. Possibly help Quint too.

From what she could tell over the deployed airbags, the windshield appeared to be intact. That was probably a good sign. She craned her neck around, trying to get a glimpse into the back seat.

"Quint," she said a little louder this time, a little bolder.

Through the windshield, she saw flashes of light coming toward them. The SUV?

"Quint," she repeated for the third time as hopelessness threatened to swallow her whole. There was no way she would leave her fiancé in the back seat and take off. Ree scrambled to find her cell phone. The contents of the vehicle had been scattered around like fall leaves in north Texas after a violent thunderstorm.

His non-answer sent her pulse racing as the flashlights picked up the pace.

Chapter Eleven

The sounds of a familiar frantic voice cutting through the fog in Quint's brain registered as Ree. He tried to shake off the confusion, but that only made his head hurt even worse. Her voice had a distant quality, like she was standing inside a tunnel.

But that couldn't be right.

"Come on, Quint. You have to wake up. They're coming," she pleaded.

He wanted to. He also needed to know what had her so twisted up. Then it came back to him. The motorcycle. The chase. The SUV. Then the crash. He'd barely gotten his seat belt clicked when they'd swerved off the road.

There were other voices. Ones he didn't recognize, but they still caused icy fingers to grip his spine.

Quint blinked blurry eyes open. Ree was positioned over him, her gun aimed toward the voices. His head felt like it might crack into a thousand pieces at any moment, but he couldn't give in to the fog rolling over him and through him.

A half-dozen thoughts competed for attention,

but there was only one he would allow to surface. They needed to get the hell out of there. The Chevy's front and side airbags had probably saved their lives.

"Ree," he said, and could hear the raspy quality to his own voice. He coughed a couple of times before he realized the reason for the sudden dryness. "Fire."

"You're awake?" The shocked quality to Ree's tone said he'd been out far longer than she was comfortable with.

"I'm here. Something's on fire," he said.

"Let's climb out the back," she said. "Can you move on your own or do you need me to help?"

Quint stretched his legs out as far as he could given the fact he was on his side in the SUV. He removed his seat belt, releasing the cutting pressure running diagonally across his chest. He was already pressed against the door. His hip dropped, smacking against the armrest. He ignored the shooting pain and scrambled onto all fours.

"Lead the way," he said to Ree before realizing his Sig Sauer was around somewhere.

"The flashlights are getting closer," Ree said. "I'll see what I can do to hold them off."

She disappeared out the back of the vehicle as Quint felt around for his weapon. A few seconds later, the sound of a bullet split the air. A flash of light came from the back of the vehicle before there was shouting. The voices were male, and he was able to detect two distinct tones. It looked like they were evenly matched. He liked those odds, especially with a crackerjack agent like Ree on his team.

Everything outside of the Chevy went quiet, save for the sound of the blaze that was growing by the second. The glow from the fire gave him some light to work with as he crawled around. He needed to get out of there before the fire spread to the gas tank or lines.

He was about to give up and abandon his gun when his fingers touched the cool metal of the barrel. He stretched them around the driver's seat where the gun had ended up on the floor and retrieved the weapon. Their odds of survival just increased dramatically with this find. To be fair, Ree was doing an excellent job of holding off the attackers.

A returned shot had him scooting out of the back of the vehicle at lightning pace. It was pitch black in the area surrounding them, so he had no idea what they were about to run toward. The only thing for certain was he needed to get them away from the burning vehicle and the roadway, which meant heading into the blackness.

Quint checked his back pocket for his cell phone. Relief they'd won the first battle washed over him. They could use the phone to navigate out of wherever they were about to end up. *If* they had cell service, a voice in the back of Quint's mind picked that moment to say.

It was true. Still, he'd take having his cell over losing it any day.

"Do you have your personal belongings?" he asked Ree.

"I have my Glock," she stated. "Having my purse would be nice, but I didn't think to grab it."

She was most likely focused on saving his backside, and that was the reason for the slip. He owed her one for that.

"Looks like we have a little time before this thing blows. I'll grab it," he said. "Hold them off just like you're doing and I'll return before you know it."

Ree opened her mouth to protest, but he was already climbing in the back of the vehicle. There was enough light for him to locate her handbag a whole lot easier than his gun, which had been wedged between the driver's seat and the door.

The fact Dumitru had played them in the worst possible way and then gotten away sat hard in Quint's gut. This was the equivalent of shoving Quint's nose in his mistakes.

This wasn't the time to chide himself for losing the bastard. What was done was done. There was no going back now. Eyes forward, Quint grabbed Ree's handbag and retreated to the back of the SUV in time for another round to be fired.

The gunfire was returned. A bullet pinged off the Chevy not two feet away from Ree. He grabbed her and pulled her out of harm's way in time to shield her from the next one.

They fell into a heap on the hard Texas soil.

"We need to run," she said. "Can you?"

Quint performed a quick mental inventory of his body.

"I'll figure it out," he said. His headache alone was enough to slow him down. There were other ailments that—thankfully—the recent boost of adrenaline would handle.

"Let's go," she said, securing the strap of her handbag over her shoulder. She didn't wait for an answer as they both ducked as low as possible to make them harder targets to hit and took off in the opposite direction of the highway and into the blackness.

The rolling hills were a stark contrast to the flatness of Dallas. The farther they ran from the Chevy, the thicker the underbrush became. The toe of Quint's boot got caught on it, causing him to faceplant. Ree came down with him. Both held on to their weapons. The accidental move was probably where their luck would run out as a pair of bullets whizzed past their heads. Falling had narrowly saved them.

They lay there for a long moment, heaving, trying to quiet their own breathing so they could hear how close the attackers were. Something had been bugging Quint about the motorcycle incident. Had they jumped to a conclusion that Dumitru was the rider?

The sobering thought they'd been led here to be killed nailed Quint. After his exchange with Lindy, anything was possible. Lindy might have decided the organization didn't need Quint. Had he and Ree acted too quickly in spying on Lizanne's place without a solid plan?

Other thoughts raced through his mind, but those had to be shelved for the time being. He'd analyze the situation once they were clear of danger. Considering another set of bullets split the air, they needed to get out of there.

"We're being too predictable," he whispered through labored breaths. "We need to zigzag our way toward safety, heading that way," he said, pointing to what he believed was northeast.

Their eyes had adjusted to the light enough to see objects right in front of them.

"Hold on," Ree said, squeezing his fingers. "Okay. Now, let's go." She hopped to her feet at almost the exact moment the Chevy exploded. Gas and fire weren't exactly the best of friends.

The blaze caused enough of a distraction for the two of them to make it out of the firing line. A couple of wild shots were fired, but Quint could easily see they were out of desperation and not because the shooters had either of them in their sights.

The hills seemed to roll on forever in this area. Quint had hoped they would make it to trees at some point. Those would be useful for cover and would make shooting them a whole lot more difficult. At least they still had weapons and cell phones. That should help with escape and eventual recovery.

Bjorn wasn't going to be thrilled with what had just happened to the Chevy. Quint wouldn't need to quit when this case was over. She would string him up for the cost of the vehicle.

When the only thing they could hear was the whisper of the wind, Ree stopped and plopped down.

"Stay low, just in case," she said, tugging his hand so he would sit down beside her. She located her cell phone, saw that she had a couple of bars and called 911.

He listened carefully for the sounds of footsteps while trying to catch his breath. He wasn't out of shape, but this case was threatening to do him in. He'd been beaten within an inch of his life and was still recovering. He'd been slapped around more times than he cared to count. The battle scars were racking up. Normally this run wouldn't have winded him to this degree.

Could he keep his strength up long enough to make it through the night and get answers?

A VEHICLE SQUEALED off in the distance, and that was the first time Ree really breathed. Thankfully, this area carried sound. The second exhale came when she heard sirens, which she prayed weren't just ringing in her ears from the crash.

"Do you hear that?" she asked Quint.

"I sure do," he confirmed.

"I'm guessing that's the reason the bastards took off," she said.

"Either way, the blast probably just saved our lives," he pointed out. She couldn't argue there.

"We should make our way back to the Chevy," she said, "or what's left of it."

The red glow had disappeared after they'd climbed and then descended the most recent hill.

Quint pushed up on his elbows as the sirens grew closer. He leaned over and kissed Ree in a manner that was so tender it robbed her of breath.

"What was that for?" she asked when they finally pulled apart.

He shrugged his shoulders.

"It was just something I needed to do," he said.

Ree's heart squeezed in her chest at the sentiment. She'd felt a wall come up between them after their last talk. One that wasn't completely down yet. This was a start.

She urged him to his feet, realizing he'd taken a pretty hard tumble inside the Chevy as it had rolled. He squinted and winced as he pushed to standing.

"Are you okay?" she asked.

"I'll be fine," he reassured her. "This body has been taking a beating on these cases. I'm ready for it to be done."

She couldn't agree more with the sentiment.

She asked the question that had been bugging her. "It wasn't Dumitru. Was it?"

"I don't think so," he confirmed.

"Any ideas who, then?" she asked.

"My mind immediately snaps to Lindy," Quint said, returning his Sig Sauer to his ankle holster. "The way he looked at me earlier was murderous. If Dumitru really was in the apartment, Lindy would have lost face big time. It could cause him to seek revenge. This certainly sent a message to us both."

"He's definitely on the list," Ree remarked, putting the safety on her Glock before tucking it into the compartment in her purse made for an easy concealed carry. "But something in your voice tells me that you're unsure."

"Lizanne might have good security. Our Chevy

might be more recognizable than we realize. Anyone at the top of the organization could have us followed," he said. "Here's the thing. Lindy didn't have to let me walk out of the apartment today. I took a risk once I let him up from his vulnerable position on the balcony. He had a couple of guys there who could have followed me outside and done a number on me. They didn't."

"Which could mean he didn't want your killing tied back to him," she reasoned. Quint had made a lot of good points. But their thinking might be too narrow. Like a scientist who came up with a theory, and then all his thinking and evidence afterward built a case to prove it. Consciously or subconsciously. "What else?"

"This could be protection for Lizanne," he stated. "We must have been caught casing the place, and whoever was inside might have believed we were out to rob her or make a hit on someone."

"I was thinking the same thing. Lizanne and her people definitely go on the list," she said. "We can ask Grappell to get any and all information about her background, where she likes to eat and where she lives. That kind of thing. He has plenty of resources in the office at his disposal to help him dig around."

Ree reached inside her purse to check for the replacement cell phone and found it. She fired off a text to Grappell and found out there was no cell service.

Quint scratched his head, wincing the second he made contact.

"How is your vision?" she asked Quint, redirecting the conversation. She didn't want to think about Giselle right now. Not when Ree was still so angry at the woman she could barely see straight.

"It's fine now," he said.

"Do you know what you hit your head on?" she asked.

"It all happened so fast," he said.

"We can ask for a medic once we get back to the Chevy," she offered. They probably should get him cleared medically. Bjorn would ream Ree out otherwise. Not to mention the fact Ree was concerned about how much Quint's body could take. Granted, he was strong and fit. He had muscles and stamina for days, but he wasn't twenty any longer. He'd taken a lot of hits over the course of three cases. Now, they were on their fourth with no break in between. The speed had been necessary, but that didn't mean it was good for his longevity. In fact, they were in more danger with each passing day. Plus the list of people they'd angered was growing. The fake killing of Vadik should have bought them more time.

A thought niggled at the back of her mind. Was there another player involved? Someone they'd miscalculated or overlooked? Crime organizations weren't exactly known for recruiting decent and honest people.

"With all the arrests, the ranks might be getting itchy to make a name for themselves," she said.

"There could be a power struggle going on,"

Quint agreed. "It would explain why someone wanted Vadik dead."

"You said 'someone,'" she pointed out. "Does that mean you don't believe the order came down from Dumitru?"

"I have questions," he stated.

Chapter Twelve

Now that the discussion was gaining steam, Quint's mind was going down a very different path. He didn't trust Lindy or Giselle as far as he could throw either one of them. They clearly knew each other, though, because they'd been working together to kidnap and bury Ree.

As they neared the Chevy, a fire truck blasted the area with water. They gave it a wide berth as they linked their fingers.

"We should hold our hands up so no one gets too anxious about us popping up from nowhere," Ree said.

They did just that as a sheriff came around the side of the vehicle with a searchlight.

"That's our vehicle, sir," Quint stated. "We were going a little too fast and took the corner too hard."

He didn't want to give away their identity to the sheriff, and he figured he could play the victim pretty well. They should be done with this and on the road back to Dallas in fifteen minutes.

The sheriff was tall and looked exactly like the

cliché one would think of coming from Texas. He was dressed in tan clothing from head to toe. His belly hung over an oversized belt buckle, and his crooked nose was a little too big for his face.

"I'm sorry, sir," Ree picked up when the light burned their eyes. "I was driving, and I got distracted. My fiancé hit his head."

"Tell me what you two were doing out here alone so far away from your vehicle, and don't leave out any of the details," the sheriff said without introducing himself. Some of the sheriffs in Texas got their jobs through connections and intimidation rather than by popular vote. Quint imagined it happened in every state on some level, but it practically burned him to pieces this was happening here. This sheriff could very well be one of them.

Quint didn't normally like to give himself away, but one glance at Ree said she was already thinking the same thing. Of course, their badges were locked in the tackle box back at the apartment, so they couldn't exactly prove they were law enforcement.

"Sir, I'll tell you what," Quint began. "Since you didn't seem to feel the need to identify yourself or take that blinding light out of our eyes, I'm going to ask you to call my boss instead."

"And who might that be?" The sheriff sounded incredulous, like he couldn't believe they were trying to pull one over on him.

Quint evaluated his options. It was possible someone from the crime organization had ties to the community. Doubtful, but he'd already made an assumption that got them in this position in the first place.

"You know what?" he said. "On second thought, let me tell you what happened from the beginning without leaving anything out."

"Go on," the sheriff said, lowering the searchlight enough for Quint's eyes to stop seeing stars.

"My fiancée and I were getting a little frisky while she was driving," he began. Ree shot a hard look at him, but he continued, "She doesn't like talking about our sex life with strangers."

Ree's fingers tightened around his.

"It was my fault," Quint continued. "I couldn't wait until we got to the hotel room. Our GPS flipped out and kept wanting us to drive in circles." He threw his arm around Ree's shoulders. "And we just got engaged recently."

The sheriff scowled.

"The two of you need to come with me," he said.

This was highly unusual and unprofessional, and there were a few choice words Quint wanted to throw out right about now. Instead, he clamped his mouth shut and nodded.

"Step apart and walk over to the fire engine," he said. "Spread your legs and put your hands on the vehicle."

"Are we under arrest, Sheriff?" Ree asked in an innocent tone.

"Not yet," the sheriff responded.

"Okay, but you should know we're both carrying," she said, raising her hands high in the air. "I have a weapon in my handbag, and my husband has a gun in his ankle holster."

It was legal to carry in the state of Texas, so the sheriff shouldn't have a problem with this.

He cocked an eyebrow.

"Hands against the vehicle," was all he said.

Quint couldn't wait to get this jerk's badge number and report him. If only the sheriff knew he was messing with another law enforcement agency, Quint highly doubted the man would keep the smirk on his face, a smirk Quint wouldn't mind personally erasing.

Bjorn wasn't going to be thrilled with the phone call she was about to get, Quint thought as he complied with the sheriff's request. After being patted down and having his gun confiscated, he was seriously ready to throw a punch.

"I need to make a call," Quint stated, all attempts at courtesy now gone.

"I'm afraid—"

"The last time I checked, unless I'm under arrest, I have a right to make a phone call," Quint stated with a little more anger and frustration seeping in than he'd intended. "Unless you're prepared to deny me my rights."

"No, that won't be necessary," the sheriff said. "Make your call, but keep your hands where I can see 'em. And hand over your IDs first."

"You just confiscated the only weapon I have on me, and, meanwhile, my vehicle has just gone up in flames. So I don't exactly have any means with

which to hurt anyone," he quipped. Ree fished her
license out of her purse as Quint pulled his out of his
wallet. They handed them over, and then the sheriff
disappeared into his vehicle after a stern warning
that they shouldn't go anywhere.

Where did he think they were going to go in the
boondocks without a car?

Ree shot Quint a warning look the second the
sheriff's back was turned. She was right, though.
His temper was flaring dangerously close to out of
control, and he needed to rein it in.

Quint white-knuckled his cell phone. He didn't
look forward to the behind-chewing he was going to
get from his superior, but Bjorn would lose her cool
on the sheriff first and would back Quint to no end.
He was confident in that fact. She wouldn't rip him
a new one in front of this jerk of a sheriff.

He took a deep breath and faced the music, tap-
ping her number into the cell. Bjorn answered on
the second ring. And, yes, she'd been dead asleep.

"What is it?" she asked, voice stern.

"We're in some Podunk town being held by a
sheriff with no cause and he won't properly identify
himself or give us a badge number," Quint stated.
"We need your help."

"What a jerk," Bjorn said.

"You got that one right," Quint agreed.

"I was talking about you," she quipped, leaving no
room for doubt she didn't appreciate the middle-of-
the-night interruption. That was fine. Quint wasn't
exactly in a cheerful mood either.

"This one is not on me," he stated.

"Where are you?"

"Your guess is as good as mine," he stated. Then whispered, "We were run off the road. This guy is harassing us, full tilt."

Bjorn cursed. She was protective of her agents and wouldn't take this news lightly. He hoped it would soften the other part he was about to tell her. Giving the boss a heads-up was always about delivery more so than the message.

"Are either of you hurt?" she asked.

"We're fine," he said.

Ree moved next to him and said, "Not exactly. Quint's hurt."

"What? You buried the lead, Casey. How bad is it? How many resources do you need?" she asked rapid-fire. He could hear her scrambling to get out of bed. Bjorn's reaction was over the top, especially for her. But then, this case had had a dark cloud hanging over it since day one, and she'd seen him after the last beating.

"You're talking to me, right?" he asked. "So, I'm alive."

"That's a good place to start," she said on a sigh. "Where are you hurt?"

"Head took a blow. Had a little blurry vision. I'm better now," he reassured her.

"So, I'm hearing you had a concussion," Bjorn stated.

"Not this time," he countered. He'd had enough to know the signs.

"Well, that's a relief," she said, and he could hear the release of some of the tension in her voice.

"Chevy didn't fare so well," he stated, figuring it was safe to deliver the news when her guard was down.

The string of curse words she released would have made a sailor blush.

"And I'm hearing that you don't know where you are. Is that true?" she finally asked. "Not even a general idea?"

"We were headed from Dallas to Houston. Hold on," he said as Ree touched his arm. She had her own cell phone out and was using the map feature to figure out where they were.

She gave him the exact coordinates, which he immediately relayed to Bjorn.

"I'll have to take a second to look that up to figure out whose jurisdiction you're in," Bjorn said. Knowing her, she slept with her laptop on her nightstand. It didn't take long for her to identify the county they were in along with the name of the sheriff. "I've had reports on this imbecile before. Not only is he incompetent, but that makes him dangerous."

"Doesn't sound promising," Quint stated.

"Don't worry. I'll take care of him. It's high time he was put in his place." The line got quiet for a stretch of a few minutes while the sheriff sat in his vehicle, calling in their IDs.

"Your friend is about to get a phone call," Bjorn said when she finally came back on the line. "Trust me. He isn't going to like this one bit."

"This is the best news I've heard all day," Quint admitted. And then he sat back and watched with amusement as a startled-looking sheriff took the call.

HOME. SHOWER. BED.

Those were Ree's top priorities despite the momentary distraction of watching the sheriff get his due. The man genuinely paled.

The phone call didn't take long, and he sure didn't waste any time when it ended. He was out of his SUV in a heartbeat.

"Excuse me for coming down hard on the two of you earlier," he said. "We've had a rash of..."

His voice trailed off like he couldn't think of how to finish the sentence, a sure sign he was lying. Ree clenched and released her fingers a few times, trying to work off some of the tension and frustration from the interaction they'd had with him a few minutes ago.

It was amazing what an attitude adjustment could do. The sheriff's smile was ear to ear as he handed both their identification and weapons back to them.

"My apologies about taking those," he said, leaning forward rather than stepping too close.

Ree wasn't certain what he'd been told but he now seemed afraid of them, and she didn't mind the change in demeanor one bit. It also reminded her just how powerful their boss was, considering she could make a call in the middle of the night and have a sheriff change his tune in a heartbeat.

"My name is Sheriff Rex Gunther," he said, offering a handshake.

Quint stared at the man's hand for a long moment before finally giving in and shaking. Ree was next, and she had similar enthusiasm.

"I'm at your disposal," Sheriff Gunther said. "Anything you need, you ask."

"We need a ride back to Dallas," Quint stated. "Preferably now."

"Take my keys," the sheriff said. He dug inside his pocket and tossed over the key fob. "I have a deputy on the way, and I'll be here on the scene taking detailed notes and pictures for quite a while."

"Dallas is a couple of hours from here," Quint said. "Are you sure you want us to take your primary vehicle?"

Ree shook her head.

"We can't." There was no way she was driving up in a sheriff's SUV unless she was in the back seat with handcuffs on or else she would blow her cover.

"I can arrange an unmarked vehicle," he offered before checking his watch. "I can have something here in the next fifteen or twenty minutes if you can hold tight."

"That would be fine," Ree said. "And, Sheriff, do you have an EMT available to take a look at my fiancé's head injury? He took a blow during the crash, and I want to make one hundred percent certain he gets a green light before we leave the scene. You'll probably want to put all this in your report, as well."

"I'll wake Donovan. There's no need for a report

on this one. We'll just get you checked out, set up and on your way in a jiffy," he said, holding up a hand as if to say he was on it. He had a whole lot more skip in his step now as he'd made certain an EMT was on the way to the scene. He returned with a couple of bottled waters in hand. "Would you like to wait inside my vehicle? Take a load off?"

"We would, Sheriff. Thank you," Ree said, wondering whose name Bjorn had to have dropped for this turnaround from the sheriff or who their boss said they were.

While she was at it, maybe they could get answers as to who was driving the SUV responsible for this mess.

Chapter Thirteen

"Does it strike you as strange that Giselle was working with Lindy?" Quint asked as he took a seat beside Ree in the sheriff's vehicle. Sheriff Gunther stood a few feet away, talking on his cell.

"Now it does," Ree said. "In all honesty, she has been bothering me in general since the whole 'tricking me outside' scenario, so I'm probably not the best one at being diplomatic when it comes to her."

"No one blames you for wanting to wring her neck," he said.

"She showed up at our apartment, looking for someone to protect her," she stated. "The woman was ready to throw herself at you."

"With Axel in prison, it is more difficult for him to protect her," he said.

"We all thought he arranged for her to be with Vadik after going inside," she stated. "What if she did the same thing with Vadik?"

"Went in and basically threw herself at his mercy while also playing Axel?" Quint asked.

"She would be smart to hedge her bets," Ree pointed

out. "The world she lives in could crumble down at any moment."

"We could go have a conversation with Axel about Giselle," Quint stated.

"Yes, but he might tip her off," she pointed out. "We have no idea what he knows about her current life and he is still doing his best to protect her. Even by placing himself in harm's way."

"He might have been the one to instruct her to go see Vadik and ask for help initially," he reasoned.

"But what about Lindy?" she asked. "I just don't see these guys looking out for each other's girlfriends."

"Lindy used you to get to me," Quint said. "With most organizations, girlfriends and wives are off-limits no matter how bad the conflict within becomes."

"We've already seen this one break that boundary with Axel's wife and kid," Ree said. "Maybe I should have seen my kidnapping coming."

"Don't do that," he said. "Don't condemn yourself when I'm just as much to blame as you."

"You weren't the one who ran outside the minute Giselle wanted to meet," she pointed out.

"True, but that doesn't mean I'm without blame," he said. "I should have been there to protect you. I wasn't."

"You can't be everywhere," she whispered as the sheriff walked toward the vehicle.

"Donovan is about three minutes out," Sheriff Gunther informed them. "He'll drive you wherever you need to go. That way there'll be no need to worry about arranging for a pickup. I know him personally. He's a good guy."

"Thank you," Quint said. They could get a ride downtown and have Donovan drop them off a couple blocks from their apartment. It was safer that way. He didn't mind the sheriff's buddy knowing the general area, but there was no need to be dropped off at the front door.

"You should know Donovan won't say a whole lot so as not to make you feel uncomfortable," the sheriff explained.

"Good to know," Quint said. Ree was quiet. He could almost see the wheels turning in her mind, churning over their conversation about Giselle.

True to the sheriff's word, Donovan arrived exactly three minutes later. All conversation between him and Ree stopped with the sheriff standing within earshot. Donovan looked to be in his late twenties. He had a short, stocky build and gave the impression he'd probably played football during high school. He had a square face and a boxer's nose. He came toward them with his hands out wide, away from his body, carrying a medical bag.

"This here is the patient," the sheriff explained, motioning toward Quint.

Donovan's serious expression never faded as he gave a nod before setting down his bag and then opening it. First he took out his stethoscope. "Are you experiencing any dizziness?"

"No," Quint stated.

"Blurred vision?" Donovan continued in his all-business tone.

"Not since right after the accident," Quint admitted.

"How about your head? Any pain there?" Donovan asked.

"I have one helluva headache," Quint said. "Nothing I haven't dealt with before, though."

"Okay. I'm going to flash a small light in your eyes and take a look. Okay?" Donovan asked.

Quint nodded and blinked the minute the light hit his retinas.

"Sorry about that," Donovan stated.

"The light hurts. I have a minor headache. What are we talking about here? A mild concussion at best?" Quint laid it all out.

"Sounds like you've been down this road before," Donovan said.

"I played sports growing up," Quint explained. "And then there are job hazards."

"Understood." Donovan finished his exam. "I agree with your assessment. You need to rest and drink plenty of fluids. Avoid screens if at all possible."

Compared to the head injury he'd sustained on their last assignment, this was nothing. Still, the damage was piling up.

When they were finished with the lecture, Donovan asked, "Are you ready to go?"

"Yes, we are," Ree answered, and he realized how tired she must be. "And if we can stop off for coffee so I can make it back to Dallas, that would be great."

"I'll see what I can do," Donovan promised. He seemed a little too quick to want to please Ree, and that got underneath Quint's skin. He reached out and took her hand in his, linking their fingers as they walked over to Donovan's dual-cab pickup. It looked comfortable enough inside.

Once Ree was seated in the back, Quint said, "Why don't you rest your head on my shoulder and sleep on the way back to town instead of having coffee?"

"Are you sure?" She blinked up at him with those emerald eyes that shone like rare gemstones. As corny as it might sound, it was easy to get lost in those eyes.

"I got this," he said. Besides, he wanted to think a little more about how Giselle and the others might be connected and, more importantly, Ree needed to rest.

Ree leaned against him and, as it always did when she was this close, the world righted itself for a moment.

"I love you," he whispered, and was rewarded with a smile he couldn't see so much as feel. That was Ree. She had an affect on him no others could touch.

"Where to?" *Donovan* asked.

"Downtown Dallas." Quint rattled off the cross streets two blocks from their apartment. It was as close as he wanted the EMT to get to their actual address. They could easily walk from there.

Donovan entered the streets into his GPS and navigated onto the highway. The young man kept his eyes on the road in front of him and the vehicles around them.

The steady hum of the road lulled her to sleep a few minutes after they reached the highway. Quint's thoughts rolled back to the start. Who had been on that motorcycle? How was Lizanne involved with Dumitru? Were they business associates or something more?

The motorcycle had been too far away for him to get a picture of the license plate. He could kick himself for not trying when it was in the parking lot. Although, to be fair, if Dumitru had been on the bike, it wouldn't likely register back to him officially.

The rider had been dressed head to toe in white. Who did he think he was? The Milkman? Milkman knew how to ride, that was for certain. At the speeds he'd been going, he would need a handlebar stabilizer on the type of bike commonly referred to as a crotch rocket. Quint's mind was drifting, so he brought his thoughts back into focus.

Milkman was smart. He'd checked to see if they were following him, and then he'd called for backup. But why? Did he recognize Ree and Quint? The thought didn't sit well. It was possible he was used to watching out for a tail, which meant he was involved in illegal activity up to his eyeballs. Then again, that was a given. Did this mean Lizanne was dirty too? She'd been running a legitimate business for years on the surface at the very least. Would she jeopardize her livelihood? Or had she been dirty all along and was just that good at hiding it?

Vadik had cooperated, and he was the reason they'd made it this far. A lot had happened in the past forty-eight hours. Quint generally needed to mentally shut down at some point in a busy day to process everything. Ree had already sent Grappell a text asking him to check into Lizanne's background and business. The agent was a miracle worker, so Quint hoped they would have information about her by lunch tomorrow.

Considering it was almost 2 a.m. and they'd been in a car crash, Quint figured both of them could use a day to sleep in. It wouldn't hurt to take a couple days off in order to gather intel and study the situation. They were moving too quickly and impulsively. Granted, his instincts were normally dead-on, but this case was different, and they'd been under for a long time. Fatigue was an issue, mental and physical.

Jazzy, his mentor, used to tell Quint to rest when he was tired, not quit. Bringing his grades up after goofing around for years had been a challenge. Without Jazzy's guidance, there was no way Quint would have graduated high school let alone be where he was today in his life and career. Jazzy retired from police work and now spent a whole lot of time with a fishing rod in his hand. Quint needed to give him a call.

Since his thoughts were bouncing all over the place on the ride home, he made a mental note to circle back to Axel. The two needed to have a conversation about Giselle without Quint showing his hand. He wanted to get a sense of whether or not Axel believed the woman could survive on her own.

Another thought struck. She'd come to his apartment to offer herself up in exchange for protection.

Was she trying to get close to Quint to figure out what had actually happened to Ree? Giselle could have been sent in to cozy up to Quint so she could spy on him and Ree. There were a whole lot of men who would have taken her up on the offer. She'd insinuated sex came with the bargain. That, and subservience. The thought made his stomach churn. He couldn't imagine being with any woman who wasn't an equal partner in every area of their lives. Anything else would make him feel like a creep. The whole idea of using a powerful position to get what someone wanted from the opposite sex was no longer acceptable. A new dawn was on the horizon, and Quint welcomed it. Because it meant having real conversations with a partner. It meant sharing responsibilities. Quint didn't need a mother. He'd had the best, and she'd done everything in her power to ensure he turned out to be a good man. He hoped he would have made her proud if she was still alive.

Once again, his thoughts drifted to how much he wished his mother could have met Ree. The two would have gotten along well. His mother had a heart as big as the Texas sky. His father had broken her spirit, so he'd had a ringside seat to the kind of damage a terrible partner could do. Was it the reason he'd been so careful with his own heart?

For a while there, he'd all but given up on finding someone as special as Ree. Children had never been a consideration for him or for her until she'd gotten pregnant.

Quint exhaled slowly and pinched the bridge of

his nose to stem the headache. He'd refused any medication earlier and now was wondering how smart a decision that had been. He'd pulled the tough-guy routine when he probably should have accepted help. Why was it so hard to admit he wasn't indestructible?

He thought back to his childhood, and the tough exterior he'd put on like armor. He'd gotten into his fair share of trouble. Shame still cloaked him over the way he'd treated his single parent mother when she'd needed him to step up.

Going back in his thoughts always filled him with regret. Thankfully, she'd lived long enough to see him turn his life around and get through high school. His mother had died way too young, and he realized now that she'd lost the will to live working odd jobs to keep the family afloat. She'd gotten him through school and not much more. She'd helped him cross the finish line and get started on a better life. There wasn't a day that went by he didn't think about her and her many sacrifices. If she were alive, he would buy her the house she'd never had. His mother didn't talk about her own childhood much, but Quint always had the impression hers wasn't great. His father was supposed to be her ticket out of poverty when, instead, he left her holding the bag with their child and all the expenses that came along with having one.

Speaking of single mothers, he couldn't help but compare the ones he met to his own mother. Giselle was the exact opposite. Rather than be with her kid, she was out partying with a criminal ele-

ment. Quint's mother had been beautiful by most
standards. She could have ditched him and hooked up
with another guy after her husband walked out. He'd
overheard her on the phone one day explaining her
lack of a dating life to one of their distant relatives
over the holidays. She'd said there was no way she
was bringing home a stranger while she had a young
son in the house. Was she afraid all men were like
Quint's father? That they'd take what they wanted
and leave her?

He couldn't ask those questions now. All the time
he'd lost with her while he was out making trouble
filled him with more regret. If he'd stayed home, he
could have gotten to know her better.

Either way, she'd still been an angel walking on
earth in his eyes. Nothing like Giselle, who seemed
ready to throw herself at any man. Nothing like this
woman who seemed eager to let her sister bring up
the boy she claimed to love. Did she even visit him?
Did he even know who his mother was? Or was her
sister bringing him up as her own child with Giselle
out of the picture?

Another thought struck him while he was on the
topic. Did Giselle get pregnant in order to trap Axel
into support and protection? It seemed possible. Desperate people did desperate things, he thought. And
yet, no matter how desperate his mother had been,
she'd always walked the line of honesty. At one time,
he'd convinced himself that she was living in a fairy-
tale world when she told him to keep his nose clean,
his eyes open and his heart kind. He'd thought she

was one step away from being committed. Honesty and kindness weren't the norm on the streets where he grew up. His mother had been a bright light in the eye of a storm. She had somehow remained calm despite having their electricity shut off on more than one occasion. She had somehow kept her dignity when they only had hand-me-downs to wear. She had somehow managed to keep her chin up, at least around him. He'd overheard her crying into her pillow one too many times. It woke him up and caused him to decide to hold up his end of the bargain.

If Quint could go back, there was so much he would change with regard to how he'd treated his mother during his dark years. Funnily enough, she would have forgiven him in a heartbeat, told him he was just learning what not to do, and then given him a big hug. Why was it so hard to forgive himself?

Chapter Fourteen

"We're here." The voice startled Ree awake. She'd been sleeping so deeply, slobber dribbled down the side of her mouth. There was something about being with Quint that had a way of making her feel safe.

"Are you awake?" Quint whispered, and his voice was a low rumble in his chest.

She lifted her head and wiped her mouth with the back of her hand before nodding. It was probably a good thing there were no mirrors around, because she probably looked like a hot mess. But the couple of hours of shut-eye did make her feel surprisingly rested. Muscle stiffness following the crash was a whole different story but she could cope with it.

"I am now," she said with a smile. Looking up at Quint, she saw the tiredness in his eyes. There'd been no way he would have allowed her stay awake while he slept, so she didn't push the issue. He would have wanted to ensure there was no damage from the concussion, and she'd respected his need to stay awake and focused. "How much does your head hurt?"

"Believe it or not, it's improving," he said.

She studied him as *Donovan* pulled over onto the side of the road.

"Liar," she said.

"I never said you had to believe it," he quipped. He was being a funny guy to distract her from the fact he was actually in pain. Not a good sign. She wouldn't call him out on it. All she wanted to do was get him home and to bed.

"Thank you for the ride," Ree said to *Donovan* after rolling her eyes at Quint.

"You're welcome," he said with a smile and a courteous wave.

Ree climbed out of the back seat and onto the familiar road two streets over from home. She took Quint's arm and wrapped it around her shoulders, partly because she wanted to be close to him and partly because she wanted him to be able to lean on her if he needed to.

Quint thanked *Donovan*, as well. The man made a U-turn and split so fast Ree's head could spin.

"Ever see someone so happy to be rid of two people?" she asked Quint, figuring she needed to keep the topic light. Her fiancé and partner had no doubt been going over details and thinking about the players nonstop, trying to figure out what they were missing.

"Can't say that I have," Quint fired back. He stumbled but regained his composure quickly. Adrenaline had long since faded, and they were at the mercy of their bodies at this point. Between the crash and the long drive home, he had to be exhausted.

"Same here."

The closer they got to the apartment, the more Quint seemed to lean on her. By the time the elevator dinged, indicating they'd arrived on their floor, he was basically sleepwalking.

"Straight to bed with you the minute we walk through that door. Got it?" she said with a stern look before cracking a smile.

"You wanting to take me to bed isn't exactly going to cause any argument from me," he stated. Good to know his sense of humor was still intact.

"Not tonight, tough guy." She closed and locked the door behind them, half expecting Giselle to jump out from the door to the stairwell before they'd made it inside. Of course, she had to know Ree was back by now. Lindy would have mentioned it. Ree was still trying to wrap her mind around the two of them being in league.

"Since I smell like…" Quint made a show of lifting his arm and making a face.

"You don't stink, but I think you were about to say that you needed to take a shower," she said. "Make it quick, mister."

"Have I told you how much I like it when you boss me around?" Quint teased. He was half-drunk with sleepiness. The tired had officially kicked in, and Quint's brain was leaving the building.

"Hurry up and I'll help you undress," she said with a wink.

A man had never raced to the shower faster.

She could pick his brain in the morning or afternoon, whenever they managed to wake up. Quint wasn't the only one in need of a shower. She could probably use a good night of sleep too, but she wasn't sure if that would happen now that she'd had her power nap. Napping had two outcomes with Ree. It either energized her or made her feel like she was walking around outside of her body for the rest of the day. Normally she didn't risk it because she never could be certain which nap would show up.

Ree joined him in the bathroom, mainly to keep an eye on him. As tired as he was, she couldn't risk him taking a fall in the shower and cracking his head again. He seemed to have skated without a serious head injury from the crash, and she wouldn't tempt fate twice. She was, however, grateful for the person who'd invented seat belts and the person who invented airbags. Both were the reason the two of them had walked away from what should have been a fatal accident.

Quint turned on the spigot and let the water heat up while she helped him undress. The man was perfection if ever there was a perfect body. She noted the scars too. The places he'd been stabbed and where bullet fragments had nicked him. He'd been lucky so far. Her only fear was that the luck would run out before this case could be put to rest.

"I spent the whole ride home thinking," Quint finally said after stepping into the water and closing the glass door to the shower.

"I figured as much," she said. "What did you come up with?" She didn't want to go into it too deeply before they slept, but curiosity was getting to her.

"My mind keeps going back to Giselle and wondering if she is as innocent as she seems," he said.

"Mine too," Ree confirmed.

"And I can't figure out what Lizanne would have to gain by exposing her legitimate business to a criminal," he continued.

"She's either in a relationship with Dumitru or protecting him," she said. "He could also have something on her and be forcing her to cooperate. These bastards take what they want and have no regard for others."

"I was thinking along those same lines too," he stated. "Think we can have a discussion with Axel about Giselle?"

"As long as we're not obvious about it," she reasoned. "Maybe we can have a face-to-face with him and say we're checking on him and his family. We can even pretend to be bringing him information about Giselle. Say we're worried about her and that we're doing everything to keep her safe. He might not tell us the truth, but his reaction will give us some information to go on."

"I agree on all those points," he said.

It was impossible not to watch him in the shower. He made something as simple as washing himself look graceful. No, *graceful* wasn't the right word for Quint. Although he did have an athletic grace about him that was downright sexy.

They talked about mostly mundane topics for the

rest of his shower. When Ree was reassured he'd be fine putting himself to bed, she took a turn. There was something nice about washing the day off her before bed. The warmth of the water soothed her aching muscles.

The hard object that smashed into Quint's skull could very easily have nailed her instead. She could have lost Quint if his head had been positioned a little to one side and his temple had been struck instead of the back of his head. She might have been hit just as easily. It was dumb luck that had the object smashing into him and not her.

Her first thought was her mother. What would happen if Ree died? She'd been too young to remember many of the details of when her father passed away but had overhead her mother speaking to Ree's grandfather one night about it. Her mother had been crying, something Ree rarely ever saw her mother do. Her grief had spilled out of her eyes, and she'd talked about the last words she'd had with her husband before he left for work that day.

Regret was powerful. Was that the reason her mother had always kept Ree at arm's length? Was her mother afraid of getting into another argument right before Ree walked out the door? Was that the reason the woman had an almost permanent scowl when she looked at her daughter? Wouldn't she want to hug Ree tightly every day before work instead, just in case? Or could her mother not even go there with something actually happening to Ree?

Seeing regret eat Quint from the inside out helped

Ree realize just how powerful remorse was. When this case was over, she needed to talk to her mother. Between now and then, the words would probably come to her. Right?

After her shower, she climbed into bed with Quint. He was already in a deep sleep. She didn't care. All she wanted to do was curl up against his warmth. The thought of how fragile life truly was had stirred a place deep inside her chest. A thought surfaced. Had she ever gotten over the loss of her father? Had she ever given herself a chance to grieve? Or had watching her mother's sadness imprinted on Ree?

Those were the thoughts spinning around in her mind as she gave in to sleep.

They'd been asleep for a solid eight hours when pounding on the door caused her to sit bolt upright. Quint snapped into action, throwing off the covers, stumbling around a couple of steps as he hopped into his jeans. Ree wasn't much better as she managed to slip into yoga pants. The T-shirt she slept in would have to do as she retrieved her Glock and followed her partner to the door.

He checked the peephole, took a step back and then shook his head. He mouthed the name *Lindy*.

Ree reached for the knob, but Quint put a hand on her arm to stop her. Heart beating against her ribs, she held her breath.

"We need to talk," Lindy said through the door.

Was he checking up on them to see if they'd lived after last night's crash? The Chevy wasn't in the garage downstairs. But then, it seemed like he already knew.

"Are you home?" Lindy practically shouted. He was loud enough to disturb a neighbor who opened their door and asked what the hell was going on out there.

Ree released the breath she'd been holding when she heard Lindy mutter a curse word before stomping away toward the elevator. The man had a temper, which probably shouldn't come as a surprise.

But what was the visit all about?

QUINT DOUBLE-CHECKED to make sure Lindy was gone. He was in no mood to deal with that sonofabitch.

"It's clear," he said to Ree.

She exhaled and secured her weapon back in her holster. He did the same, and then they both placed their guns inside the closet for safekeeping.

"What the hell did he want?" she asked, but the question was rhetorical.

"I'll check my phone in a minute to see if we had a warning before he showed up," he said. The clock on the wall read eleven-thirty. His body cried for more, but he could get by on what he'd gotten.

"You look much better today," Ree said to him before walking over and giving him a kiss.

"I feel it," he said after bringing her into an embrace. "A couple of muscles are screaming at me, but my headache is basically gone."

"That's good news," she said. "I'll freshen up and make some coffee."

He watched as she disappeared into the bathroom, thinking he was the luckiest man on earth. This case would be behind them before they knew it, and she would be making wedding plans. He didn't mind leaving the details up to her. He already had everything he needed once she'd said yes to his proposal. The rest was just paperwork and formality as far as he was concerned. He was still bouncing all around at the idea of children, one minute thinking he could do it and everything would magically be okay and the next wondering if his father would pass down his miserable genes.

Rather than waiting for Ree to make coffee, Quint made himself useful and started brewing a pot. After his turn in the bathroom, they worked side by side in the kitchen, toasting bagels and slathering cream cheese and jelly on top.

By the time they sat at the counter, they had gotten down a couple of bites of their breakfast and a few much-needed sips of caffeine. He could take an over the counter pain reliever once he had enough food in his stomach. That should help with the residual soreness, whiplash and muscle aches.

"How are you feeling, by the way?" he asked Ree.

"Like I got in a car crash last night," she quipped.

"When we're done eating and checking phones and emails, we both need a couple of ibuprofen," he said with a smile.

"No argument from me there," she said, stretching. It looked like her left shoulder caught as she raised her arm. "I'm feeling the creaks and groans hard today."

"We've earned a day off," he said.

"It would be a good idea to take stock of what we already know and try to put some of the puzzle pieces together. At the very least, we can lay everything out and see where we end up," she responded.

"My mind was spinning way too much to be able to sleep until we got home and my head hit the pillow," he admitted. "Now that I have some caffeine inside me, I'll check to see if I have any messages."

It was probably good they didn't respond to the "emergency"-sounding bangs on the door. They'd caught Ree off guard with the text from Giselle that begged her to meet for lunch. There was no way Quint planned on falling for the same kind of trick again. Slow and methodical would be his mantra from now on. It was too late in the game for mistakes when it was clear someone was willing to kill off anyone who seemed to get in the way or threaten the operation.

He glanced at his screen. There were messages, all right. His gaze landed hard on the last one from Lindy.

"Giselle has gone missing," he said to Ree.

"She was trying to keep me alive and now…"

Had Giselle come to him because she knew something was about to happen?

Chapter Fifteen

"Giselle looked and acted desperate when she came here yesterday to ask for my help. You're not the one to blame for whatever's happened to her." Quint made sense, and yet guilt still ate Ree alive.

Since sitting around stewing over what they could have done differently wouldn't change a thing, she threw aside her regret before it had a chance to take hold.

"I'm guessing Lindy thinks we had something to do with her disappearance," Ree commented.

"His tone does give me that impression," Quint stated.

"This looks bad," she admitted. "At least, to an outsider."

"Or someone in law enforcement," he added.

"Or someone on the inside of a crime ring," she continued.

"She could have gone into hiding of her own volition," he reasoned.

If she truly had been in danger and was down to begging for protection, she might have stepped on more toes than theirs. Since the organization was showing signs of cracking under pressure, the higher-ups might be looking for targets or anyone they deemed as someone who might talk in the case of an arrest.

"After she came here, she might have figured the best way to stay alive would be to get off the grid for a little while at the very least. Wait until things blow over," Ree said. "It's exactly what I would do if I was in the same situation."

"We were attacked and Giselle has gone missing all within a twenty-four-hour period," Quint pointed out.

"Hold on," he said. He pulled up a contact on his phone and made a call. "Ree is here with me. Mind if I put the call on speaker?"

There was a short pause before Grappell's voice was on the line.

"Ree?" he said.

"I'm here," she confirmed.

"We've been worried about the two of you," Grappell scolded, his voice the equivalent of her fifth-grade schoolteacher's. It made a cold chill race down her back.

"Sorry," she said. "I just saw your texts. Sounds like you have information about Lizanne."

"That's correct," Grappell stated, a little less schoolteacher and a little more agent-like. "Her real name is Loraine Ridden. She started out as a stripper in a club near White Rock Lake fifteen years ago, and that seems to be where she met several members of Dumitru's organization. Although the ties are murky like pretty much everyone else we try to investigate in this case. At least we know Lizanne's birth name and age. She's now thirty-eight and considered attractive by most standards. I sent over another picture of her back then and now."

Ree checked her phone and then held up the photos so Quint could see them too.

"She looks a whole lot like a young Anna Nicole Smith in the early years," Quint pointed out.

"And probably more like the famous ex-stripper than she should in her older years," Ree said. Lizanne had breast implants that made hers too large for her frame and bleached blond hair styled similarly to Anna Nicole's. The resemblance probably helped Lizanne become very popular in the Dallas strip club scene, where big boobs and bigger blond hair meant raking in the cash.

"Lizanne had made enough money by age twenty-five to start her lingerie business," Grappell mentioned. "She has to have some business savvy in order to achieve a successful enterprise."

"Or, like in many cases, a very wealthy hacker," Quint said.

"She hails from Blum, Texas," Grappell continued after agreeing to Quint's statement.

"Now, there's a small town," Ree said.

"Population of less than five hundred residents," Grappell informed them.

"How is that even possible?" Ree asked, thinking there should be a minimum number of residents before a place could call itself a town.

"I grew up in a small, boring town outside of San Antonio," Agent Grappell said. "It wasn't right for me. There was nothing to do unless you enjoyed bonfires out by the lake, underage drinking, and the big highlight of your night was cow tipping."

"Sounds awful," Ree said. "Don't get me wrong, I love a good small town, but there needs to be shopping nearby, restaurants and things to do on the occasional night out."

"Same, except for the shopping bit," Agent Grappell said.

"Well then, it's possible she had stars in her eyes from a young age and would have probably been bored to death in a small town with so few distractions," Ree said. She laughed. "My family would have taken up half the population."

"Wouldn't the entire town be related?" Quint quipped.

"Scary thought and probably not too far off base," Ree confirmed. It might be a nice town to grow up in, but young people would have to move if they wanted to go to college or work in most professions after high school other than ranching. The latter wasn't a bad life, but it wasn't the one she'd signed up to live.

"Lizanne's connections to Dumitru must go back a long way," Quint stated after a thoughtful pause.

"Or she could have gotten her seed money from someone else," Ree said. "An older gentleman who likes to frequent those types of establishments. Someone with money like the oil guy Anna Nicole married."

"We could be looking at this the wrong way. What if Lizanne was the one to help Dumitru?" Quint reasoned.

"It's good to pick this apart from all angles," Ree agreed. Divergent thinking had helped solve many cases in a world where the norm didn't seem to exist any longer. Despite her observing the men in A-12 to be chauvinistic, it could be a mistake to paint them inside a box and leave them there. Who knew what the true boundaries were anymore?

"I'm afraid public records aren't a huge help there. Not without a subpoena," Grappell stated. "We'll keep digging until we've checked every last resource to see what we can find."

"Your efforts are much appreciated," Quint confirmed.

"We couldn't do what we do without your expertise," Ree stated, adding her two cents for good measure. It wasn't a huge shock the two of them agreed on almost everything. What had been a surprise was just how much they'd clashed on their first case together. Their chemistry or whatever it was called had been white-hot. Combined with the fact she'd been a bundle of nerves over working with a legendary agent despite being fully capable herself, and there'd been sparks between them from the get-go. Sparks that had led to a slow-burning flame she prayed would never go out.

Being with Quint she'd experienced the hottest

kisses, the absolute best sex and, yes, the best conversations in her life.

The image of him naked in the shower from last night put a smile on the corners of her lips despite the serious focus on the case. It was impossible not to grin a little bit when she thought about how well the two of them fit together in bed and out.

There was only one thing standing between the two of them heading into their future with open arms and making their life plan…this case.

"I think that is about all I have to contribute for now," Agent Grappell said. "I'll let you know when I come up with anything else."

"Thank you," Ree said at the same time as Quint.

"Lindy thinks we're involved with Giselle's disappearance," Quint stated.

"He said that?" Grappell asked.

"In so many words, yes," Quint said.

"Be careful," Grappell warned.

"Always," he said. Now it was time to put their heads together and figure out their next step. "Can you dig up Giselle's sister's address? We need to swing by and see if the kid is still around."

"Will do," Grappell said before he promised to text as soon as he had it.

"Shouldn't take him and the team long to find that," Ree said. "We probably have time for another cup of coffee."

They also needed a vehicle if they were going anywhere, but the look on Quint's voice said her other thoughts could wait.

QUINT POURED A second cup of coffee for Ree before refilling his own mug. He grabbed a couple of ibuprofen for her, then filled a glass of water. Once Ree had downed hers, he followed suit. Twenty minutes was all it would take for the pain relievers to kick in. His body felt rough on a good day after the beatings it had taken over the years.

"Hey," he said. "I know we're focused on the case right now."

"Sometimes changing the subject and *not* thinking about it brings the best results," she reasoned.

He couldn't argue with that logic considering he was about to say the same thing.

"I do realize I've been going back and forth on a topic that I think has become important to you, and it could impact your happiness in a future with someone like me," he began. This probably wasn't the time or place to think about starting a family, but he was still on the fence about it, and he needed to know if his position was a deal breaker for her.

"Are you referring to having children?" she asked.

"Thinking about Giselle's relationship with her son—" he paused " or should I say non-relationship, had me going down a bad path." He needed to get this out, and then they could swing by Giselle's sister's house to see if the boy was still there or if Giselle had ditched town with the kid. The thought of either didn't sit well because if she took the kid, then she was in real trouble. This wasn't the topic at hand, and he was letting his mind wander because he didn't know how to approach talking about what had been on his mind. "I'm not sure how I feel about reproducing or extending my genetic line."

Ree sat perfectly still, hands in her lap, a look of compassion on her face. It wasn't anger, so he'd take it.

"Here's the thing. I want you to have everything you want," he continued when she didn't immediately respond. What could she say? He'd just dropped a bomb in her lap. He hadn't seen the kid thing coming, which was stupid on his part. He should have realized someone with a big family might want to have kids of her own.

"I already do," she said after a thoughtful pause.

"What if I'm not enough?" he asked, his pulse racing like he was asking out the prom queen.

"You are," she confirmed, and he really believed she meant it.

"That might be true now, Ree. But what about in the future?" he asked, but it was a rhetorical question.

She sat there, perched on the stool. Her lips were compressed like when she was thinking hard about a topic or searching for an answer she knew was there if she concentrated hard enough. He loved knowing these little things about her.

"Let me ask you a question," she began after a long pause. "Last week, did you know you were going to be in a car crash yesterday?"

"No, of course not," he stated, not sure where this was heading.

"Me neither," she continued like her thoughts were

the most logical things. "Do you know what last night taught me?"

He shook his head.

"That not everything can be planned for. I mean, you do your best in life, and then there's just this whole big piece that no one can predict and no one can plan for. You know?" Her forehead wrinkled, and she pursed her lips.

"Life is unpredictable," he conceded. "I'm not sure what that has to do with me denying you children if you want to become a mother, and I can't get there in my mind. That's a big topic that some would definitely view as a deal breaker."

"It is a big deal, and it surprised me when the thought basically attacked me," she admitted. "I never considered children before I met you, and now that's changed. Some might say it's wholly unfair to you to do an about-face like that."

"How could you have known how you felt before it hit you?" he asked, and then her point smacked him square in the chest with the force of a bomb detonating.

"I know two things for certain in life right now. The first is that I want to marry you. You're the one for me, Quint. It's just you. That's all I need. The other is that I need to find a way to forgive my mother and let her know that we're okay. After worrying about you, she was the first person I thought about after last night's crash," she said on a sigh. "I have to make that relationship right or I'll never be able to forgive myself if something happens to her."

Quint walked over to his bride-to-be and brought her into an embrace.

"I know that I love you more than life itself," he said, wishing this could somehow be easier and that he could just promise her the moon. He *wanted* to give her the stars and the whole sky. And yet he knew himself, and he was having doubts about the whole family bit. "I've never said that to another person, and I know I'll never find someone like you again if you walk out of my life."

"That can't be what you want, Quint," she said, and he could hear the hurt in her voice. Hurt *he* put there. Hurt he couldn't erase.

"It's not. There's no question in my mind that you're exactly the right person for me. You're all I need," he said. "I feel complete. But you don't, and that's where the complication comes in."

"I didn't know it would happen," she said, and when she looked up at him, her emerald eyes were shining with tears. He hated to be the one to put them there. "And I never said you weren't enough."

"No, you didn't." He didn't put up an argument. There was no use. He could tell by the resignation in those eyes that she knew they'd hit a wall in their relationship too.

"What we have is better than anything I've ever experienced," she continued. "And I might want kids right now, but who knows if that will change by tomorrow?"

They both knew it wouldn't.

"I don't want to lose what we have, Quint," she said. Those words nearly broke his heart.

How could he stay with her and force her into a life she might not want? And how could he leave her and shatter both of their hearts?

Chapter Sixteen

Ree could live without kids. Right?

Before she could get too involved in the thought, her cell buzzed. She picked it up and checked the screen.

"We have an address," she said to Quint. "Now all we need is transportation."

Quint retrieved his cell phone as the conversation they'd been having came to a standstill.

"It looks like we have a Jeep downstairs. Keys are inside underneath the driver's seat," he said. Then he stopped and looked at her like he was looking through her. He was the only person who she would swear knew what she was thinking. "Are we okay?"

"I told you that I love you and my future is with you," she said. "I needed you to know that I was at the very least thinking about what it would be like to have a family with you and whether or not that seemed like something I would want. Turns out, it is. But we don't have to have all the answers right now."

The look in his eyes and the way his jaw muscle

ticked planted a seed of fear deep inside her that they didn't see their futures in the same light.

"You deserve the world, Ree," he said, locking gazes with her. There was a storm brewing behind those gorgeous sapphire blues.

They had to be able to work this out. She couldn't allow herself to believe this would be a showstopper for either one of them.

"And so do you," she pointed out before standing up, pressing to her tiptoes and kissing him.

He teased his tongue inside her mouth, and a thousand campfires lit inside her, warming her, drawing her toward their light. She could stay like this forever. Quint was enough. Kids, in this moment, were optional. However, he had made a good point. Would she regret not having them?

It didn't matter, she thought as they broke apart. She loved this man. She planned to make a life with him. And, besides, who really knew if kids were in the cards anyway? She could want them until the cows came home, but what if she physically couldn't? She'd been in relationships. Granted, she'd been careful. There hadn't been any surprises over the years despite no method of birth control being absolutely foolproof.

Ree was getting older too. At this point, she didn't even know if she could have children. Her eggs were, like, ancient in egg terms. So he could be concerned about something that might not even be possible.

The only things she knew for certain were that life could be unfair and unkind. It never made a promise that tomorrow would come or the next day. It didn't promise a rose garden. And it didn't promise that all anyone's wants would be met. People lived happily with far less than what she and Quint had between them. Besides, she had a niece and a nephew. Her other brothers would have kids at some point. Men weren't bound to the same biological clock as women anyway. Her brothers could have kids well into their forties. For women, the statistics weren't so great.

"I'm pouring a to-go cup of coffee after I get dressed since I didn't finish my second one and now it's cold," she said to Quint. "Do you want one for the road?"

"No, I'm good with this one." He picked up his cup and polished off the contents. He made a face that told her just how cold the coffee had become.

Ree wasn't an iced latte type, and neither was Quint. Despite the heavy mood, his reaction was priceless.

After retrieving their weapons and getting dressed for the day, they headed downstairs to the garage and the waiting Jeep. When something like this happened, there was always the fear one of the folks they were after would question them having a replacement turn up so quickly. But then, it seemed like pretty much everything could be ordered and delivered in twenty-four hours or less from the internet. However, their cover story of Quint coming out of prison and them staying in a borrowed apartment only went so far. They were supposed to be broke. The SUV was long gone, and they could always say they sold it for the Jeep if push came to shove, she guessed.

"How far away is the address?" she asked as they climbed inside the Jeep. The ibuprofen was doing its job at least. She was in considerably less pain than earlier unless emotional scars counted, and those were racking up today. She hadn't meant for the "having a kid someday" conversation to turn into the possibility of a breakup. Life could deal some really interesting twists.

Rather than stew over it, she realized Quint would have to come to his own decision about moving forward with their relationship. There wasn't anything she could do to stop him if he wanted to throw what they had away. And she understood on some level that what she'd been asking might rattle him. Given his past, the thought of kids wasn't on his radar.

Then there was Tessa and her baby. Was he still blaming himself for their deaths? It would be just like Quint to convince himself that he didn't deserve a real family after Tessa's death. Logic flew out the window in times like these, even with intelligent people, people like Quint.

The thought she might have just destroyed an entire relationship over kids she didn't even know were physically possible struck hard.

Ree shelved the thought as Quint pulled up the address on his cell phone.

"It's an address in Frisco, so looks like we'll take a straight shot down the tollway and exit on Eldorado Parkway," he said. "Considering it's the afternoon, we should avoid any heavy traffic. I'd say we'll be at their door in half an hour or less."

Ree checked his phone. He wasn't kidding about the residence being a straight shot. Once they got off the tollway and onto Eldorado, they needed to hang a left and then drive a couple of blocks to the neighborhood on the right before Teel Avenue. Easy peasy.

They sat in silence on the ride to the suburbs. A few cloud rolled by, and the sun was buried behind the swaths of gray. While a population of less than five hundred was definitely too small for Ree, the suburban sprawl seemed worse. There might be pizza delivery and more restaurants than any one person could feasibly cover in a lifetime around this area, but the utter lack of space in between houses made her feel claustrophobic.

Exiting the highway, they made a left and then a few minutes later pulled into the neighborhood of newish houses that all pretty much looked the same to Ree. Small front yards. Manicured landscaping. Cookie-cutter houses. Definitely not her taste, although she liked the fact they were new. The neighborhood lacked the tall trees she was used to on her own property—a property she'd seen far too little of in the past couple of months. She was beginning to miss home from a place deep in her soul.

The only thing that would make her home better was having Quint there full-time.

"What's our cover?" she asked as Quint turned onto Giselle's sister's street. She'd been so caught up in her own thoughts, she'd forgotten to ask the family's names.

"I think we go to the door as a sales team," he said.

"What exactly are we selling?" she asked, wondering if people went door-to-door to sell anything these days considering everything was a click away on the internet.

"Educational services," he said after scanning the homes. "These look like people who would spend their money to help their kids get ahead in life, so I'm thinking we pretend we have a new business and are trying to let local folks know about it."

"What kind of educational services?" she asked, thinking the man was a genius and could read a room like nobody's business.

"SAT prep or math tutoring," he said after a thoughtful pause.

She shivered.

"No one wants to learn math from me," she said, making a sour pickle face. "Plus, won't we need a flyer or something?"

"We can ask if anyone in the home is getting ready for high school," he said. "This seems like a neighborly community. I'd bet they would be willing to hear about a neighborhood business opening. All we have to say is that we're having mailers printed and will be sending those out but wanted to stop by and meet as many folks as we can on a personal level. That will be our marketing ploy. We are different from the competition because we get to know the family and we care."

"Wow. Remind me to ask you for help when I develop the next big thing and need to get the word out," she said in appreciation. He could actually make a living at this whole marketing business.

His smile caused more of those campfires to light inside her chest.

"I used to sell stuff in my youth," he admitted.

"Drugs?" she asked, shocked.

"Baseball cards," he countered. "And shame on you for thinking I was a druggy."

"I never said you were," she shot back. "I only mentioned that you might have sold them. There's a huge difference. In fact, one of my friends went into the police academy. He flunked out, or so everyone believed, and then he was back on the street working a normal job. He was also selling pot, but it turned out that he was actually undercover, had graduated first in our class, and he couldn't tell me until six months later when the busts had been made. As it so happened, he sold drugs in his youth without ever touching them for himself."

"How close are you with this 'guy'?" Quint made air quotes around the word *guy*, suspicion obvious in his tone.

"What? It was a million years ago," she said defensively. It was impossible to be mad, because it was adorable when he was jealous. "And I can be friends with guys, you know."

He seemed to catch himself when he smiled.

"Yes, you can," he said. "I just hope this guy knows his place with you."

"You're missing the point of the story," she quipped.

"Oh, right," he said. "And that was?"

She playfully slapped his arm. "The point is that you don't have to be a 'druggy' to sell drugs. Some people see it as a business transaction or a way to make easy money if they are reasonably smart or have fallen on hard times."

"Or they could sell baseball cards," he said.

"True enough. But is there the same demand?" she asked.

"That's what develops the sales skills," he said. "When you have a product not everyone realizes they need yet."

"Good to know that you're not just arm candy," she teased, appreciating the lighter conversation. They needed to switch gears and get back into work mode. The whole baby and family conversation had thrown her completely off track. "Ready?"

Quint pulled in front of the home that looked more like a mini-mansion. Ree wondered who needed this much space. She preferred cozy over what had to be room after empty room. No matter how many kids she and Quint might have, she wanted to live in her place even if it meant crawling over each other at times. And if there were no kids, the place was also perfect for her and Quint. Not too big and not too small. Not an inch of wasted space or money. It warmed the practical side of her that knew what it was like to grow up without a whole lot of extras. Her family wasn't broke, but her mother had worked hard to support them after losing her husband.

"You should talk if Giselle's sister answers," Ree said. She figured there weren't many women who would even listen to what was coming out of Quint's mouth, as gorgeous as he was.

"And what if her husband answers?" he asked.

"I'll take that one," she offered. "But what if Giselle is here, hiding?"

It was a possibility, however slight.

"I don't think she is," he began. "And here's why. This is the first place anyone who knows her would come. In fact, we'll have to be careful because of it. She might warn her sister that if anyone or anything seems weird, the woman should call 911 immediately. I'd prefer not to have another scrape with the law on this case if at all possible."

"Same here. In fact, I'm still trying to figure out whose name Bjorn dropped to get that sheriff to stop giving us a hard time and instead practically volunteer to fix us tea and fluff our pillows at night," she said.

"Fluffing the pillows is a little dramatic," he said on a chuckle. Joking around eased some of the tension that came right before facing an unknown event or outcome in a case. It was good to calm the nerves.

"I'll give you that one," she said. "So, what are we walking into here? What's Giselle's sister's name? I get that she's married with kids of her own. How many? And do we know what ages?"

Quint studied his cell phone.

"Her sister's name is Nicole, and she's married to a guy by the name of Terrence." Quint scrolled down with a flick of a thumb. "They have two kids who are both school-age. The boy is in fifth grade, and the daughter is in third. Nicole married up the social scale and into a little bit of money."

Ree glanced at the clock.

"Looks like the kids will be getting out of school in the next hour," she said.

"Let's hope Nicole is home," he stated.

"We already know Giselle's son's name is Axel," Ree supplied.

"That's right," Quint said. "Now, let's go see if the little guy still lives here."

"She might have taken him with her," Ree said.

"I'm thinking Giselle most likely took off in a big hurry if it was her choice to disappear," he stated. "I doubt she had time to fill her sister in on who might show up at the door looking for Axel. She might tell her to be careful or not to open the door to strangers."

"Right," Ree said.

"Which brings up another good point. Someone might have already been here," he said.

"And they could still be watching the house," Ree stated.

"Then we probably shouldn't sit here for long," he said before exiting the Jeep. He came around to her side and held out a hand as she exited.

Ree took the offering, hoping they weren't walking into a trap.

Chapter Seventeen

Ree kept her head down as she walked up the sidewalk to the two-story mini-castle. She glanced over at Quint as he brought his fist up to knock.

"Promise me you'll never want to live in one of these," she whispered.

He chuckled, but the enthusiasm about their future was gone from his eyes, and that scared her more than anything else they might face today.

Quint knocked on the door, then rang the bell for good measure.

"Who is it?" a female voice Ree assumed belonged to Nicole asked through the door. A shadow passed behind the peephole.

Ree nudged Quint into the woman's view. He had a way of getting doors to open once women got a good look at him. She also reached for his hand once she saw Nicole's reaction to his face in her portal.

"Hello, my name is Quint, and I'm here with my wife, Ree. We are opening a new business next month at the corner of Teel and Main, and we'd love to come in and tell you about it if you have a moment," he said.

Nicole's eyes widened for a split second before she seemed to pull it together enough to smile.

Ree moved into view and returned the smile. The snick of the lock coincided with the word, "Sure."

The solid mahogany door opened enough for them to get a good look at Nicole.

"Come on in and tell me about your new business," she said.

A TV blared in the background as she led them to the kitchen and closer to the noise. A little boy with a thick black head of hair sat in the middle of the floor, entranced by the TV. There was a smattering of toys scattered around him that looked like someone had overturned a box and let the contents fall where they might. The toys were all manner of bright colors, covering the rainbow.

She surveyed the area to see if there were any remnants of Giselle around like an extra purse lying on the floor. If she was there, she would most likely have hidden before her sister answered the door.

Nothing jumped out at Ree as odd.

"Your son is adorable," Quint stated as they followed Nicole to a table, each taking a seat.

"Thank you," she said with a warm smile and a wistful look. "He's not mine, though. He belongs to my..." She seemed to catch herself before adding, "...neighbor. I'm just babysitting while she works."

"Oh, that's really kind of you," Ree stated. "He is a cutie."

Nicole looked over at Axel with a mix of pride and trepidation. The contrast between sisters was striking. Nicole married money, plays tennis and has a family life. Giselle was a partier. Her hair was in a ponytail, and she had on a tennis skirt. Her nails were perfectly manicured, so they had that in common. And that seemed about it. Nicole lived a suburban wife's life while Giselle partied and spent time with criminals.

"Tell me what kind of business you're starting," Nicole stated after asking if they wanted a cup of coffee. They both declined. "And please tell me it's not another nail shop or day spa. We have too many of those as it is."

Nicole was what Ree would describe as chesty with a little too overly tanned skin. To the point it had an orange glow. She had long fake lashes shading light blue eyes. All in all, she would be considered attractive by many people's standards. Ree was more the flannel shirt and jeans type of person. What nature gave her, she was stuck with because she had no plans to go under the knife for a bigger bra size or to change her appearance in any way. Even her tiny early wrinkles were badges to her. She'd smiled a whole lot to earn those babies.

"No, nothing like that," Quint started, taking the lead. It was for the best since Nicole seemed distracted by his good looks. "We're offering SAT prep for high schoolers and tutoring for anyone who needs a little help."

"Oh, that sounds wonderful," Nicole piped up. She seemed to sit up a little straighter as he spoke, causing her ample chest to thrust toward him.

Ree had to stop herself from making a snarky comment and refocus. She used the time to look around as though she was admiring the decor. One entire wall was covered with an array of crosses in different shapes and sizes. There were professional quality photos of her two children over the fireplace mantel along with another one of the whole family together. Everyone wore jeans and a white shirt.

There didn't seem to be any pictures of the sisters together or of the bigger family. The little boy was still focused on the TV. It didn't appear that his mother had been in the room a few moments ago. And there was no immediate evidence Giselle was hiding out here. Again, the odds of her doing that were probably slim.

Should Ree and Quint be concerned that the woman didn't seem to have spoken to her sister? If she had, Nicole would likely have been far more suspicious of her and Quint showing up randomly at the door. She most definitely wouldn't have invited them in. So, no, Giselle didn't seem to have warned her sister.

Then again, she might not have wanted her sister to worry. It was possible Giselle got herself into something she couldn't easily get out of and decided to disappear for a couple of days to let it blow over. At this point, they'd only ruled out her being here.

As angry as Ree was with the woman, she genuinely hoped Giselle hadn't been taken or disposed of. The thought caused a cold shiver to race down her back. In this world, anything was possible. Plus, these guys didn't seem to hold women as sacred as some other criminal organizations did.

Quint finished his sales pitch about their fake business while Ree stared at the little boy in the family room. Something funny happened on TV, because his face broke into a wide smile.

"You two planning on starting a family soon?" Nicole asked, breaking into the moment.

"How do you know we don't already?" Ree asked.

"Oh, I just saw the way you were looking at my... at my neighbor's little boy. I recognized that look." Nicole practically beamed when she referenced Axel despite the almost-admission he was her nephew. Ree couldn't help but wonder if Nicole knew who his father was and what kind of life her sister truly led. Then again, maybe it was best not to ask too many questions when it came to family.

"He's adorable, but, no, we aren't planning our family right now," Ree said. "We're just now planning the wedding."

"I call her my wife because we've been together for a long time and, in my heart where it counts, she already is," Quint explained, and Ree realized her slip.

"And we hope you'll visit our business when your kids are old enough to benefit," Ree continued, trying to draw attention away from her mistake. "We consider our customers family and would love to help your children meet their college goals."

"Sounds good," Nicole said with a big smile plastered across her face. "College is so competitive these days. These guys will probably need all the help they can get in a couple of years." She waved her arms in the air and blew out an exasperated breath.

Ree had no idea what the college scene was like. It felt like a hundred years since she'd gone. The admissions requirements must have gotten out of control, though. She'd heard about all the entrance scandals that had come to light with famous folks and company CEOs trying to buy the way in for their children.

"That's what we're here for," Quint said. "Since we're not opening for another month, we haven't received our business cards yet. Would you mind helping us spread the word around the neighborhood in the meantime?"

"Not a problem at all," Nicole said. "My dry cleaner is over there, and I know exactly the area you're talking about. That's a great location, by the way."

"We hope so," Quint said. "We're planning on putting our heart and soul into this business, and we hope to be able to serve the community."

"That's so sweet of you," Nicole said, and Ree was certain the woman blushed. Not that she could blame her. Quint had that effect on the opposite sex. He was good-looking beyond words and had that rugged sex appeal that was so magnetic, it had its own orbit. "Do you live around here?"

"We're building a place off of Legacy," Quint stated. His comment received a nod.

"It doesn't surprise me. Although I thought they'd found every nook and cranny to put a house out that way by now," she quipped. Nicole stood up, so

Ree and Quint followed her lead. "Welcome to the community."

"Thank you," Ree and Quint said in unison.

"Anything I can get for you guys before you leave? A bottle of water?" Nicole asked, glancing at the time. She gasped, but the little boy was too entranced in the TV to notice. "I need to give little Ax his snack before I put him down for a nap."

"Thank you for your time," Quint stated, extending a hand Nicole seemed all too eager to shake. "You've been very helpful."

"Anytime," she said with a smile. The woman blushed.

Ree would have to get used to it. She couldn't believe the two of them wouldn't be able to work out the differences over whether or not to have kids. But Quint's kids, if he decided to have them, would hit the genetic lotto as far as she was concerned. It would be a shame if he didn't change his mind about having them.

QUINT WALKED BEHIND Ree with his hand on the small of her back. He missed the contact the minute she climbed inside the vehicle. He waited until they got settled in the Jeep and were safely on the road before thinking about speaking.

"It doesn't look like anyone is following us," Ree reported, checking the side-view mirror for the third time since leaving the small neighborhood. It was good to be diligent and cautious when it came to dealing with A-12.

"I didn't see any sign of Giselle inside the house and no signs of stress on her sister's face," he said.

"Which could mean Giselle didn't contact her sister before her disappearance," Ree said.

"I'm concerned about it, if I'm honest. Why wouldn't she let her sister know that she was about to go MIA, especially when the sister is caring for little Axel?" he asked.

"We haven't really established how often the two are in communication," Ree stated. "Giselle doesn't strike me as the type who would keep to a routine like clockwork as far as visitation goes."

"That's a fair point, and now that you bring it up, I agree with you one hundred percent," he said. "It would have been nice if we could have just flashed our badges and gotten right to the point on that visit."

"Agreed." Ree leaned back in her seat and pinched the bridge of her nose.

"Everything okay?" he asked, his concern level hitting the roof as he navigated onto the tollway.

"Yes," she said. "Fine. Just a bit of a headache working up."

"It's been a while since you had ibuprofen," he realized. "Maybe the last dose is wearing off."

"Might be a good idea to take more once we get back to the apartment," she said, leaning her chair back to more of a reclined position. "I know we just ate breakfast, but I'm hungry too."

"We had mostly carbs," he said. "They run through the body pretty fast. Quick energy hit but not enough protein to last the day."

Her skin looked a little paler, but then, he didn't exactly have time to really look at her while he was driving on the tollway. It could be the lighting or the clouds that were gathering steam. Cars and trucks zipped about and treated the road like it was a raceway. He had no idea why this was, but the threat of rain in Texas caused drivers to lose their minds. Why? Driving in rain wasn't all that drastically different than any other weather condition. The main requirement was to go a little slower and be a little more careful. Why was that so difficult?

"I'm kind of nauseous, actually," Ree stated.

"Do you need something?" he asked, realizing there wasn't much inside the Jeep to work with if she needed to empty the contents of her stomach.

"Maybe we could pull over?" she asked. "Get off the road for a second."

"Yes, sure. We have time," he said, immediately navigating off the tollway and to the nearest parking lot.

"Do you feel sick at all?" she asked.

"Me? No, I'm fine. Why?" he asked.

"I was just wondering if maybe something we ate this morning was bad or past the date," she said as he hooked a right into the closest lot. He pulled into a spot as fast as he could. One look at Ree and he wondered if it was fast enough. She practically bolted out of the vehicle and to the nearest trash can.

Quint rushed to her side, rubbing her back as she emptied the contents of her stomach. A flashback to doing a similar thing to Tessa before she'd announced her pregnancy news suddenly hit him.

Tessa had made an excuse, something like bad food, as well. Was there any chance Ree could be pregnant? She would have told him. Wouldn't she? There was no way she would hide the information from him and try to pass this off as a stomach virus or bad food if she didn't get her period.

A knot tied in Quint's gut. Could this be the reason Ree had been mentioning kids out of the blue? Was she testing the waters to see what his reaction would be?

For a split second, Quint thought he might actually join her in getting sick. There was no way he was ready to be a father. He was, however, ready to be Ree's husband, as long as she didn't want kids. Quint could admit that wasn't exactly fair. They hadn't really talked about having a family together before the engagement but, again, wouldn't it be the next logical step for any couple?

All thoughts of the case flew out the window as he watched Ree retch. He felt helpless as he stood there, rubbing her back, wishing he could somehow make her feel better.

"What can I do?" he asked.

She shook her head and continued until there couldn't possibly be any bagel left inside her. She'd probably thrown up all the coffee too.

"Water?" she asked.

"There's none in the Jeep. Will you be all right

if I run over to the convenience store real quick?" he asked. There was one anchoring the parking lot.

"Go ahead," she said, but he hated to leave her out in the open like this, vulnerable.

"You're sure you'll be okay?" he asked.

"I'm good. I'm done. I'll just wait inside the Jeep while you go inside," she said.

"I promise to be right back." With that, he took off running toward the store. The pregnancy thoughts cycled through his mind. For the second time he wondered if Ree would have said something if she was pregnant.

A thought struck.

Did she even realize it herself? Or was it so early in the process she hadn't figured it out?

Quint bought the largest bottle of water he could find and made the jog back to the Jeep in record time, his heart battering the inside of his ribcage. Ree was in the seat, leaning back with her arm over her eyes.

"Here you go," he said as he slipped into the driver's side.

Ree took the offering, then opened her door after washing out her mouth. She ran over to the bin and spit.

Quint's chest squeezed as panic gripped him. All the shame and regret for letting Tessa take a bullet nearly crippled him. The memories caused the air inside the Jeep to thin. Air. He needed to be able to breathe. The simple act that he'd taken for granted every minute of the day locked up his chest. Anger and a deep sense of loss flooded him, bringing up too many painful memories from the past. With great effort, he did his best to shove those thoughts aside. Would they impact his actions in a critical moment if this case blew up?

The answer came almost immediately. They most certainly would. What the hell was he supposed to do now?

Chapter Eighteen

Ree's stomach roiled. She had no idea why. At first, she thought the food was bad. Maybe the jelly or the cream cheese she'd so generously slathered onto her bagel a little while ago. But wouldn't Quint be sick as well? He'd eaten the same things.

"The coffee from earlier just sat in my stomach," she said. "I thought I got it all out."

"I asked the clerk for a bag. He looked at me like I was losing it but handed this over." Quint produced a plastic bag.

"Thank you," she said, taking the offering. "I seriously don't know what could be wrong with me."

"Let's get you home," he said. "Think you'll make it okay?"

"I will with this," she said, motioning toward the bag before buckling herself in. She'd better not have a virus. Yes, they'd been running on empty lately, pushing themselves beyond normal physical limitations. Yes, they'd been going without proper sleep. Yes, they'd been at this for weeks on end with no real break in between.

The ride back to the building was like being seasick with no port in sight. She had the fleeting thought they should get in contact with Nicole to let her know she had likely been exposed to a virus. But without knowing what exactly was wrong, that seemed premature.

The stress of this case wore on her like no other in the past. She never would have survived as an agent this long if the cases were always so intense. The one tiny moment she'd had in between cases two and three, she'd stopped off for Sunday supper and gotten into an argument with her mother. *Fight* wasn't the right term for the standoff between the two of them.

Ree's mother had gotten in a few jabs, noting her disapproval at Ree's lack of domestic skills. Well, Ree might be getting married—at least she hoped it was still on—but there was no one, repeat, no one, who could force her into the kitchen every day. She wouldn't bake homemade pies for their Sundays either. Ree could forgive her mother for their past differences, realizing it was just a mother concerned about her only daughter and filled with regret about the husband she'd lost.

It was truly a sad situation when Ree thought about it from her mother's perspective. Unlike Quint's upbringing, Ree's had been filled with people and love.

Who did he have? He'd mentioned Officer Jazz. Then there was Quint's mother, who Ree already marked as a saint. She only wished she could have met the woman who'd brought up such an amazing human being. Quint had told Ree about his childhood struggles and the difficult time he'd had after his father had abandoned the family. Ree's heart went out to him for being an only child.

Was that the reason it was so hard for him to depend on others? Was that the reason it was so difficult for him to think about having a child? Did it have to do with his father? He'd mentioned something about the gene pool. Was he concerned his child would end up like Quint's father?

Ree could make the argument that environment was more important than having money or a pre-programmed genetic code. It probably didn't help that Quint spent his career locking away bad guys. It did have a way of tainting a person when they only ever saw the dark side of humanity. Without her family, Ree had no idea how she would stay so grounded. But there was something about being home on Sundays and surrounded by her brothers and Shane's kids that helped her stay focused, kept her eye on the prize so to speak. The whole reason she did the job in law enforcement was to lock bad guys away and keep them off the streets. As corny as it sounded, and she heard the words rolling around in her own thoughts, she really did get into this business to make a difference, as so many law enforcement officers and agents did.

Was she also there to carry on her father's legacy?

There was probably some truth to the idea. She couldn't deny that she'd never felt closer to her father than in her early days on the job. There'd been something about following in his footsteps that made her feel like he was there with her. The connection had worn off years ago, but the work was interesting and kept her challenged. She'd set goal after goal, determined to climb the ladder and be successful.

The risks were easier to take year after year. Ree rarely thought about them anymore. She'd long ago realized no one at home would miss her if something happened to her on the job. She had no kids or husband depending on her. Her mother, grandfather, and brothers would care, but it wasn't the same as starting her own family. No wonder her mother freaked out about Ree going into law enforcement. Ree had never really considered the risks from a mother's perspective. Now that she had, there was no going back.

Ree was so lost in her thoughts on the way home that she hardly noticed Quint hadn't said a word.

"I'll be okay," she reassured him, thinking he was probably just worried about her coming down with something.

She got little more than a grunt in response. The look on his face, the worry lines etching deep grooves in his forehead, tipped her off as to his stress level. Quint had a habit of getting quiet during intense times. As an agent, he was all about communication. In his personal life, not so much.

Quint parked the Jeep and exited almost immediately. He came around to her side of the vehicle before she could get her seat belt unbuckled. Ree was grateful she hadn't felt the need to purge any more of her stomach contents for the rest of the ride home.

"Do you need help walking?" Quint's concern was endearing but also unnecessary. Nothing she hadn't experienced before and gotten over relatively quickly.

Was he worried she would be down for the rest of the case? Or maybe that she wouldn't be able to perform at peak level?

"No, thanks," she said. "I'm feeling much better now anyway."

He studied her as they stepped inside the elevator. Based on his frown, he also realized she wasn't being completely honest.

"You can tell me the truth," he said. "How are you really feeling?"

"Another wave of sickness is striking. I might be coming down with a stomach bug," she admitted. The elevator dinged, letting them know they'd reached their floor. "In fact, I need to get inside the apartment fast or this elevator will forever be tainted."

Quint wasted no time dashing across the hallway and jamming the key in the lock. He easily opened the door in time for her to bolt through and straight to the bathroom. Somewhere along the way, she dropped her purse and didn't care.

Would this day ever end?

QUINT STARED AT his phone while Ree was in the bathroom. He'd already knocked and found out there wasn't anything he could do to help. *Run to the store and get a pregnancy test,* he thought. But that would be more for him than her. She seemed oblivious to the fact she might be pregnant. He wasn't.

What he needed to do was figure out a response to Lindy. The texts from him came across as desperate before. The man could truly be that clueless, or he might know exactly where Giselle was, and this was his way of trying to draw suspicion away from him. Quint had no idea what to say to Lindy at this point. Plus, he was distracted by the Ree situation.

They also needed to speak to Axel, the sooner the better.

He fired off a text to Agent Grappell, asking him to arrange a meeting. This wasn't news Quint wanted to deliver on the phone. He needed to see Axel's reaction to what was happening with Giselle when they told him. He also needed to see if, by chance, Giselle had been in contact with Axel.

The thought occurred to Quint there was some kind of turf war considering all the chaos going on in A-12 right now. The arrests seemed to be making everyone jumpy. Did they believe Dumitru had lost his touch? Or was being targeted by law enforcement? It would explain a whole lot about what had been happening in recent weeks.

Quint's cell buzzed in his hand.

There's been an incident with Axel.

The message from Grappell shocked Quint. He jumped to his feet and raced to the bathroom door. While standing there, he made the call.

"What kind of incident?" Quint immediately asked the second Grappell answered.

"He's been moved to the infirmary," Grappell said. "At this point, I'm not certain about how bad the attack was. There seemed to be a lot of confusion about what happened, and I can't get a straight answer out of the warden."

"We're heading over there," he said. "Get us inside."

"I'm not so sure that I can," Grappell said.

"Well, then use the name Bjorn dropped last night to open doors, because that seemed to work miracles," Quint insisted.

"I'll see what I can do, but there's a strict order in place for no visitors in the building after the fight," Grappell informed him.

"Do whatever you have to," Quint stated. "Just get those doors open."

"Give me ten minutes," Grappell said before ending the call.

"What is happening?" Ree asked through the door. He heard the spigot turn on, and it sounded like Ree was washing her hands.

"It's Axel," he said. "Someone made a move on him at the new facility."

"We should have known," Ree said. "We should have anticipated this after Giselle went missing."

"We don't know that the two are related," Quint said as the door opened and a flush-faced Ree stood there.

He led them back to the kitchen, unsure if it was safe for her to take anything for her stomach. They might have something in the medical emergency kit he kept in the tackle box that would help. Since Tessa had kept her early pregnancy quiet, and he hadn't exactly been around a whole lot of pregnant women, he had no idea what was allowed and what might hurt a fetus.

Bringing up the topic to Ree if she wasn't prepared for the possibility could cause her to spiral. Even if she knew on a subconscious level, she might be blocking it out. None of the scenarios were good right now. So he shelved the topic.

"He could have warned her to go into hiding. It's possible he knew someone would come after him or at the very least suspected it," she reasoned. "What about his wife and daughter? Are they still in protective custody? Are they okay?"

Quint grabbed his cell phone and started firing off questions to Grappell by text.

"We'll know soon," he said to Ree. "In the meantime, what can I get for you?"

"I wish I had some crackers," she said. "Oatmeal would be nice. I think I got the worst of it out of me."

Her skin paled, and he wondered if that was going to be the case.

"We need to speak to Axel," Ree said. "There's no way he told us everything he knew before."

"Agreed," Quint stated. "I have no idea how bad of a shape he's in."

"Then we need to get him out of there," she said with conviction.

"I don't think you can go anywhere in your condition," he said.

"I'll bring a box of trash bags if I have to," she insisted. "We have to talk to him face-to-face."

"I'm on it," Quint stated. "But I need you to feel better and not push yourself."

She chewed on the inside of her cheek for a few seconds.

"All I need is to be able to keep something down and I'll be fine," she countered. "This is just a passing bug or bad food or something. It'll be over before it gets started."

The last thing he wanted to do was upset Ree before they headed out.

"How about this…you stay here while Grappell works his magic and I run out to grab a few supplies. It can't hurt to get some chicken broth in you, and it'll take a while for Grappell to be able to arrange everything, and—"

"Oh no," Ree gasped. "We have to get him out of there. A lockdown means no one in or out. It will give anyone on the inside a chance to get to him in an infirmary, and I'm guessing that's where he is."

Quint bit out a few choice words before bringing Grappell on the line.

"Mind if I put the call on speaker?" he asked the second Grappell picked up.

"Not at all," Grappell responded.

"We need to get Axel out of prison and into WIT-SEC," Quint immediately started.

"I'm working on it," Grappell said.

"Do you need escorts?" Ree asked. "Because we're here, and we need to speak to him. This way, we could kill two birds with one stone."

She seemed to realize the impact of her word choice when she made eye contact with Quint.

"I didn't exactly mean it to come out that way," she explained with a frown, wishing she could go back and reel in the word, "kill."

"We know," Quint stated. Ree could be hard on herself. He recognized the trait because he possessed the same one.

Despite making progress on the case, he couldn't get the pregnancy question out of his mind. This was the worst time to ask, but he wasn't sure how much longer he could hold it in, either. A flashback of being in a similar position with Tessa assaulted him.

When this phone call was over, he needed to ask Ree about the possible pregnancy.

Chapter Nineteen

"As far as an escort goes, I don't know if I can get Axel out of the building, let alone have the warden trust the prisoner he's responsible for to strangers," Grappell stated.

"Could we risk telling him that we're ATF?" she asked.

"Possibly," Grappell said.

"I know we'd rather not play that card while we're undercover. It's just a thought," she said.

"How about Bjorn?" Ree asked. "She worked miracles last night. Is it possible to have her wave the magic wand to get the doors opened?"

"Not with the lockdown." Grappell issued a sharp sigh. "The US marshal in charge of his wife and daughter has just confirmed there was a security breach. He is on his way to pick up and relocate those witnesses."

"How can this be happening?" Ree asked, but the question was rhetorical, and they were all on the same page.

Frustration gave her something to focus on besides the urge to vomit that was currently taking hold. Again?

How on earth?

Ree excused herself and headed for the bathroom, hoping nothing too interesting happened while she was out of the room. She sat on the edge of the bathtub, ready for the onslaught should it come. There was literally nothing in her stomach right now, so there couldn't possibly be anything to throw up. The voices had gone quiet in the next room, but they were probably just waiting to see if she was okay. After a few minutes, the nausea eased, and she felt able to return to the living room again.

Ree checked the kitchen. Nothing. There was no one in the living room. Quint was gone.

Her cell was sitting on the counter. She picked it up, ready to call Quint and give him a piece of her mind. Anger welled up along with frustration that he would exclude her from something...

Wait. She read the text on the screen. Be right back with crackers.

Well, now she really felt bad. She'd jumped to conclusions about Quint taking off and excluding her from the case "for her own good," and he hadn't done anything of the kind. It wasn't like her to be flooded with so many emotions over something that hadn't even happened. Ree really was off her game.

This sickness or whatever it was needed to move on out of her, because she didn't like feeling this way, and she really had no patience for being sick in the first place. It made her cranky because it felt like a colossal waste of time. She'd never been the type to lie in bed all day or groan and complain about a little cough.

Of course, vomiting was an entirely different story, and she'd sworn to do that as little as possible for the rest of her life after a particularly awful experience in fifth grade. She'd mostly held to the promise and rarely ever got threw up.

By the time the apartment door opened, she felt like she'd gotten her sea legs again.

"Saltines," Quint said as he held up a box that looked a whole lot like heaven. "And a few other things I thought might help."

"You really are a beautiful man," she said.

"Hot," he corrected her with a smile that would melt ice during a Siberian winter.

"That too," she quipped, returning his smile.

"You look better," he said as he set the pair of paper bags down on the counter.

"I am," she said. "It's weird because I felt awful before you left. Must've gotten it all out before because nothing came up the last time and I started feeling half human again. A little mouthwash and toothpaste have gone a long way."

Quint pulled out a couple cans of chicken soup.

"There isn't anything we can do until we hear back from Grappell. Even with Bjorn's considerable network and resources, it might take a couple of hours before we can go anywhere. I didn't respond to Lindy yet because I can't figure out what I'm going to ask or say until we speak to Axel. So now you're caught up," he said, and she could have sworn his chest puffed out just a little bit. "Figured I might as well nurse you back to health in the meantime. I need my partner up and running, and at full capacity."

"Well, food sounds good right now. Broth and saltines are calling my name," she said, enjoying the lightness in the conversation.

Quint started pulling out supplies one by one from the brown paper grocery bag. He grabbed a bowl as he handed over the crackers.

"You might want to get started on those," he said.

"I wasn't kidding a few seconds ago. You really are beautiful," she teased. He didn't seem impressed, but she could see the small, satisfied smirk upturning the corners of his lips.

Ree couldn't wait to tear the box open and get started. The crisp crackers with just enough salt were her idea of perfection. Within minutes a can of chicken noodle soup had been heated, poured into a bowl and delivered by the man who seemed to be in a competition for sexiest man alive. She wished all her exes had realized being competent in the kitchen was so erotic. Throw in a load of laundry and she wouldn't be able to hold herself back.

This probably wasn't the right time to mention she wouldn't be against having another round of incredible sex. Quint wouldn't want to kiss her on the mouth after she'd been throwing up despite the fact she'd rinsed and brushed. The image of her bent over a random trash can earlier probably wasn't the sexiest thing he'd ever seen. So she scratched the idea of turning him on while those images might still be fresh in his mind.

Besides, the call from Grappell could come at any moment, and they would need to be ready to bolt out the door. Their window of time to get to Axel and possibly be part of his transport team might be small.

The bowl of chicken noodle soup went down great. The crackers made her feel like she might have kicked this virus or whatever.

"Has Lindy reached out to you since earlier today?" she asked.

"No," he admitted, finishing off a sandwich he'd made for himself. The thing was layered with turkey meat, ham, cheese and half a salad in between two thick pieces of bread. The only thing that could make the sandwich any better was bacon and an iron stomach. He polished off the bowl of soup he'd made for himself and brewed fresh coffee. Seeing him move around the kitchen with athletic grace, the way the cotton of his shirt stretched and released on top of his back muscles had her staring.

When he turned around, his expression sent a shockwave rippling through her. There was an uncertainty in his eyes, which were almost always sure. There was a pensiveness to his expression that warned of trouble.

"Here's the thing," he began. She was rooted to her chair in some mild form of shock with the realization he was about to say something serious. "I don't want you to panic at what I'm about to ask you."

"It's hard to agree to something when I have no

idea what's about to go down," she said, very uncomfortable with where this might be heading. Her mind snapped to too many scary places—places that were permanent and involved words like *this won't work*. Just the possibility shredded her.

"I think it's important for us to be totally honest with each other," he hedged. "I've been in relationships and friendships in the past where secrets were kept, and the damage done can be irreparable."

Ree's chest squeezed, and her heart sank to her toes.

"Okay," she conceded. "I agree that lack of honesty destroys bonds. What is it, Quint?"

"I'm not trying to be evasive," he said. "I just don't know how you're going to take what I have to say, and—"

"Just spit it out," she said, her heart hammering the inside her ribs. "When it's out there, we can decide what to do."

He issued a sharp sigh before setting his soup bowl in the sink. Then he reached into one of the bags and pulled out a box before placing it on the counter in front of her.

Once Ree read the label, she almost lost her stomach again. Not a whole lot threw her off her game. But this?

"A pregnancy test?" she asked, dumbfounded.

"BASED ON YOUR REACTION, I'm guessing you haven't considered pregnancy as a possibility." Quint hadn't been certain about the decision to put his cards on the table. But he was being serious a few minutes ago. If they were going to make a go at long term, he needed to be able to talk about everything, including the subjects he wanted to avoid.

"No, I haven't," she stated with a little more shock and indignation than he'd expected.

"Then we would just be dotting every *i* and crossing every *t*," he said. "If the possibility exists. But I haven't seen you use any products or mention anything about your cycle in a long time."

Ree hopped off the stool and retrieved her cell phone. "Hold on. I have a tracker in here because it's generally the last thing on my mind until it happens."

Quint hoped the possibility of a pregnancy didn't exist. There was no way he was ready to make the call to be a father right this minute. Not while he was still trying to figure out if he wanted children at some point later. Much later.

"Oh no," Ree stated, and her skin paled again. "That can't be."

He stood there, rooted to his spot, waiting for confirmation a pregnancy couldn't be in the cards.

"This tracker is dependent on me putting in the dates of my cycle, and we've been so busy with back-to-back cases that I probably just forgot to log it. That's all," she said, but the terror in her voice said she wasn't exactly convinced the statement was pure fact. She glanced up at Quint with the most pitiful eyes. "My recent talk about wanting children came out of the blue. I promise. I didn't have a plan for this possibility. I didn't even know it was…"

The way she stammered and seemed to search for words combined with the utter shock on her face made him feel like a jerk for bringing it up. If she was pregnant, though, they needed to know There was no way she could continue on this case.

More of those flashbacks nailed him. Tessa smiling and touching her stomach when she came to terms with being pregnant and finally told him the news. She'd also been nervous and scared, certain there was no way she could bring this child into the world and raise it alone.

Quint had promised to step up to be a surrogate father. He'd planned to be the best godfather there had ever been. He'd told Tessa that she was going to be fine and everything would end up working out for the best.

Now? All he could think was how much of a hypocrite he was for saying those things to her and then freaking out about the possibility of Ree being pregnant.

"Man," he began. "Have I been a class-A jerk."

Ree's face wrinkled as if she'd just sucked on a sour pickle. Her eyebrows drew together like she had no idea where he was going with this.

"When Tessa finally admitted to me that she was pregnant, I bent over backwards trying to reassure her that everything would be okay and she would be an amazing mother," he started as the pieces clicked together in his mind of what a true jerk he'd been in this situation. "I said everything would work out because she had me in the wings and that I wanted to help."

Ree tucked her chin to her chest in the move she did when she was getting emotional and didn't want him to see her eyes tearing up.

"I was so ready to jump in and save the day for my friend," he said.

"Best friend," Ree corrected him.

"Yes, but that's the thing," he said, coming to a realization. "You are so much more to me than that. You are my best friend, my partner, the one I want to spend the rest of my life with, and what did I say to you when you told me you wanted to have kids?"

"The situations aren't the same," she countered. "You're comparing apples to oranges."

"How so?" He was curious as to her explanation, because in his book, he'd let her down in the worst possible way.

"Tessa was already pregnant and scared," Ree reasoned. "I was talking about planning for a child. My brother Shane has two kids, and now I remember how freaked out he was when he found out his wife was pregnant with their first. He said it was impossible for him to 'plan' to have a baby, because who could willingly take on that much responsibility?"

"You thought about it and decided it might be a good idea," he pointed out.

"Not before I met you," she said. Those words were like daggers to the heart.

"Believe me when I say that I never would have asked for a family," he began, trying to find the right words. "With you, anything feels possible. If you're pregnant now, I don't want that to be a bad or scary thing, because I will always be here for you. You are so much more than my best friend and life partner. You are the great love of my life."

A tear spilled from Ree's eye and rolled down her cheek.

"I love you too," she said. "And I'd like to face whatever life hands us together."

Quint walked around the counter and to his future bride. They could do anything as long as they had each other to lean on. He kissed her, tender and slow.

When they pulled apart, Ree reached across the counter and picked up the test.

"I'll be right back," she said before heading to the bathroom.

She returned a few minutes later with the test resting on top of the box. She set it down. "Three minutes is all we have to wait now."

A whole range of thoughts went through Quint's mind, not the least of which caused a wave of panic at the thought he might actually bring a child into the world.

Quint's cell buzzed. He checked the screen.

"It's Grappell. We have to go. Now," he said.

Chapter Twenty

"What do we do about the test?" Ree figured this was how timing usually worked. The answer to the most important test of her life was minutes away and she had to leave.

"It'll still be here when we get back," Quint said as he secured his ankle holster. She followed suit, grabbing her own weapon and hiding it as they raced out the door. Not that long ago, he was concerned she'd have to get off the case if she was pregnant. The thought he could lose two pregnant partners should this investigation go south practically gutted him. Losing a pregnant best friend had nearly destroyed him. He couldn't even go there with Ree. He couldn't go to a place where she was suddenly gone along with their child.

It barely took a minute for them to hit the elevator button. The temptation to run back inside the apartment was overrun by reason. The results weren't ready, and she would be wasting valuable time. At least this way she would have time to digest the possibility of a pregnancy.

"The address is on my phone," Quint said, handing over his cell after he hopped in the driver's seat. He paused for a second. "You look better. I should have asked you before, but are you up to this?"

"I'm surprisingly good," she said, figuring that probably gave a point to "pregnant" as much as she wasn't ready to acknowledge it.

"Okay, then," he said, but his voice was anything but reassured. "Let's do this."

Ree nodded and smiled before turning her attention back to the cell phone. She clicked on the address in the text from Grappell. A map filled the screen. An address on Horton Road in Forest Hill came up. "They're keeping him in a federal facility not too far from here."

"I know that one," Quint stated. "He'll be at the medical center on Horton. Same street, but the medical building is considered Fort Worth," Quint stated.

"Axel could be recognized in this area," she said. "It was stupid to keep him anywhere near the DFW area."

"We need to have a conversation with the marshal in charge of taking care of him and his family," Quint stated. "His current location might be related to being closer to his wife and kid."

"They shouldn't be anywhere in the area either," Ree pointed out. "His teenage daughter seemed more concerned with having to leave her boyfriend than the scary people who were after her father. Besides, their brains aren't fully developed yet, and teens make all kinds of bad decisions. I'll never understand why, at the height of when their brains seek thrills, we put a driver's license in their hands."

"Our kid won't drive until he or she is twenty at the very least," Quint said. The words just rolled off his tongue like he didn't even have to think about them or their impact. Had he decided she must be pregnant? She still wasn't so sure, and they'd had to skip out on the test before the results came back. There were plenty of reasons she could be late with her cycle, not least of which was the amount of stress they'd been under from recent cases and the fact she hadn't taken a break from work yet. Her diet had been off. Her sleeping habits had been off. Her exercise routine had been off. Any one of these excuses could cause a delay. Combined, she was more and more convinced there was nothing to panic about.

They arrived in front of the medical center gates and, after a quick conversation and an ID check, were allowed inside. Aside from the tall security fences, the building and grounds looked more like a community college with its large green lawn and Spanish-style architecture.

After checking in, they were taken back almost immediately to visit Axel.

"Am I the only one who thinks it's a bad sign Axel isn't being wheeled out to greet us?" Ree whispered to Quint as they moved down the hallway.

He shot her a look that said he agreed.

They were taken to the infirmary, where Axel was lying down. Thankfully, there weren't any machines hooked up to him.

"I'll be at the door if you need me," their escort said before circling back, and waiting.

Axel was on his side. His face was swollen, bruised and cut. He groaned when he saw them, and she was pretty sure he was trying to say hello.

Quint moved to his side and squatted down next to Axel's face. Ree sat on the foot of the bed, where she could keep an eye on their surroundings and still see and hear everything happening between Quint and Axel.

"I'd ask how you're doing, but I can see for myself," Quint stated.

Axel tried to speak and coughed instead.

"Do you want water?" Quin asked.

Axel nodded.

There was a bottle of water next to the bed on the nightstand. Quint grabbed it and handed it over. "Do you want to sit up?"

He nodded. Quint went to work figuring out how to raise the bed so Axel could sip water without too much discomfort.

Ree had no idea how they were going to transport Axel in this condition. He didn't look like he could move and probably needed a nurse or doctor around just in case. But if he got a medical release, she and Quint would have to figure out how to care for him while they transported him.

Shouldn't the marshal in charge be here? She pulled out her cell phone and texted Grappell the question. His response came quickly. They'd beat the marshal to the facility.

"Listen," Axel finally said. "I have evidence against Dumitru. It's everything you want and need to convict him, lock the bastard away for the rest of his life. I kept records. There are pictures. I have evidence linking him to personally killing two of the men who used to work for me."

"Why are you telling us this now?" Ree asked. This information would have been helpful on the last case. And could have ended this whole ordeal.

"I was framed before," Axel stated. "As you both know. He was trying to shut me up. I thought if I cooperated that I'd eventually get out while protecting my family and kids, and this was my leverage against Dumitru to keep him honest. This was going to be how I got back into the money and forced him to set me up with some cash and a new crew."

Ree shook her head. Yes, she was grateful for the information. But damn, she really wished they'd known all this sooner.

"It's obvious he's going to stay at me until he kills me," Axel said. "I just want my family and Giselle to be kept out of this. Dumitru crossed a line when he started going after wives and kids."

"What do you get out of giving us this information?" Quint said.

"Safety for my family," Axel stated. "At least, I hope they can be protected. They didn't ask for any of this. They didn't know what kind of business I was in."

Ree had her doubts about his last statement.

"Where is all this evidence?" Quint asked.

Axel's gaze shifted from Quint to Ree. "It might be time to spice up your wardrobe."

Ree glanced down at the jeans and cotton shirt she was wearing, confused as to what he could be talking about.

"Not for daytime," Axel stated, and then it clicked.

"Is she involved? Lizanne?" Quint asked.

"She's been trying to shake Dumitru for the past few years, but he isn't having any of it." Axel coughed again, and this time, it sounded like a lung might come up. "He's threatening her business, and she's done. He helped her early on when she needed to get started, and he never forgot about it or let her off the hook. She runs a legitimate business and has a kid she's trying to protect."

"Does the kid belong to Dumitru?" Quint asked as Ree's gaze flew to her stomach.

"No. Nothing like that," Axel said after a few more coughs that sounded like he was hacking up another lung. "This boy is a teenager now. Him and his mother are close. She keeps him out of the family business and far away from her old life, including Dumitru."

"Why doesn't she turn Dumitru in?" Quint asked.

"Are you crazy? Go up against Dumitru? No way can she afford the backlash," Axel said. "He would send his people, like he's doing with me. I'm not even safe in protective custody." Axel coughed a couple more times. They couldn't argue with his logic.

"Where is this evidence against him?" Quint asked again.

"I already said," Axel claimed.

"Then let me be more specific. Where *exactly* is this evidence?" Quint continued.

"In the ceiling of her shop," Axel stated. "I put it there myself. She doesn't know."

"Smart," Quint said. "That way it's there if you need her to get it for you. You already know she'll help."

"True, but I didn't want to put her in the middle of this thing," Axel admitted.

"What about Giselle?" Quint asked. "How much does she know?"

"She shouldn't know anything," Axel said. "Why?"

"Because she's disappeared," Quint stated. "I thought maybe you had something to do with it."

"Oh no," Axel said, and the sadness in his voice was palpable. "How about little Ax?"

"He's fine," Quint said. "We saw him with our own eyes. Nicole has no idea what's going on based on our visit."

"Giselle can be…flaky," Axel said. "But I doubt she would take off on her own like that."

"What about Lindy?" Quint asked.

"The organization is uneasy. Folks are trying to push their way to the top. He's just as bad as the others, but he seems loyal to Dumitru," Axel said before another coughing jag. He took a sip of water.

"Where will you be safe?" Quint asked. "Is there such a place?"

Axel shrugged. He winced with the movement.

"It might be too late for me," he said. "Unless

Dumitru ends up in jail. Then I've got a shot. Lindy likes me, or he used to, and he's the next in line from all I can tell in here."

"We need to get you to safety," Quint said. "Then go find the evidence."

"There's a chance it's not still there," Axel said. Those weren't the words Quint and Ree wanted to hear.

"We'll find out," Quint said. "But I need you to call Lizanne and tell her to let us in."

"Can't you just go get it?" Axel said.

"Not if we want to use any of the evidence in court," Quint pointed out.

"Right." Axel nodded, glancing at them with a look that said it must be a pain to have to follow the letter of the law. But it was the right way to go about it. Ree never took for granted taking away someone's rights by arresting them. She had to take the bad with the good.

Quint asked the guard for a cell phone. He produced one a few moments later.

"Do you remember her number, by chance?" Quint asked Axel.

"As a matter of fact, I do," Axel stated with more than a hint of pride in his voice.

"How?" Ree hadn't meant to ask the question out loud. She was truly that shocked.

"Simple. I've known Lizanne for years, and she's on my emergency call list when I get arrested," he said. "I had to memorize her number in case my cell…disappeared."

His hesitation had caused Ree to fill in the blank with a whole different line of thought. Or should she say a whole bevy of reasons his cell might "disappear"? She could spend days coming up with ideas.

Axel punched in Lizanne's number.

"Put the call on speaker for me, okay?" Quint asked.

Axel nodded and complied.

"Hey, gorgeous," he started the minute Lizanne answered the phone.

"Axel?" There was a whole lot of excitement in her brandy-soaked voice. "Is that you?"

"It is," he confirmed. "I've got you on speaker because I'm locked up, and I have friends in the room. Okay?"

"Sure," she said, drawing out the word. "What can I do for you?"

"Give my friends a private tour of the shop," he said.

"Oh." There was a long pause. Then came, "Do I want to know what this is about?"

"It's better if you don't ask questions," Axel confirmed.

"How will I know if it's your friends?" she asked.

"They're a couple, for one," he said. "And they'll give you the code word…" Axel glanced around the room. His gaze settled on a piece of fruit on a plate on the nightstand. "Apple."

"Apple," she said. "Got it."

"Good. I'll owe you one," he said.

"No, you won't," she quickly countered. Based

on their exchange, it was easy to realize the two were friends who went way back. "But I'll collect anyway."

Axel laughed, and it caused him to bend forward to cough. When he finally composed himself, he said, "Sorry about that."

"You don't sound so good," she stated.

"I look better than I sound. How about that?" Axel asked.

"I'll wait for them," Lizanne said. "And don't be a stranger when you get out."

"I won't," Axel promised. He ended the call and handed over the cell, looking a little at a loss.

"We'll get you transported and then head over," Quint said.

Axel was shaking his head before Quint could finish his sentence. "No, sir. You have to go as soon as possible. I have no idea how long they'll leave her alone or if Dumitru has spies in here listening to everything I say. Get the evidence and arrest the sonofabitch."

All Ree could think was *easier said than done.*

Chapter Twenty-One

Quint stood at the door of Axel's room until the marshal's team arrived ten minutes later. He couldn't risk leaving Axel alone, and it gave him and Ree a chance to talk about their next steps. If Axel's claims were true and there was enough evidence to bring Dumitru down, they still had to find the man in order to arrest him. Quint caught himself glancing at Ree's stomach more than once during their conversation, wonder creeping in no matter how much he tried to keep the question at bay.

They would know soon enough, and there wasn't anything either could do to change the outcome. Worry would do no good. And Quint could tell himself the fact all day, and it still wouldn't stop the thoughts from looping. Even if Ree was pregnant, this was different. They were about to get married, and a family wasn't the worst thing that could happen to them. The thought surprised him.

Back in the Jeep, they pushed the speed limit until they reached Central Expressway and the lingerie shop.

The sun was winding down by the time they parked in front of a restaurant so their vehicle wouldn't be recognized and then made the walk over to the lingerie store in the strip shopping center. There were no cars parked out front. Quint had a feeling Lizanne had rushed out any customers who wandered inside or denied them entrance altogether.

Quint exchanged a look with Ree before opening the door.

"We're about to close," the familiar brandy-soaked voice said. The attractive woman in her late thirties came out of the backroom.

"Apple," Quint stated.

Her blue eyes widened for a split second as she took in Quint and then Ree. Keys jingled from a ring as she walked to the door. She locked it.

"I'll be in the storeroom if you need anything," she said. "My only request is that you don't trash the place while you look for whatever Axel told you to pick up."

Quint examined her posture; tension radiated from her. She was putting herself on the line for a friend, and seemed very aware of the fact.

"We'll be careful," Ree reassured her in the way only she seemed to know how. There was something about her presence that calmed others. He'd noticed it more than once over the course of their cases. She'd the same effect on him once they'd gotten over the hump of their first meeting, which had been every shade of awful possible. It was almost funny now, but hadn't been at the time.

"I'd appreciate it if you hurried," Lizanne said.

"We understand," Ree stated.

Her gaze narrowed on Ree, and then she studied Quint.

"Sorry about last night," she said. "I've learned that you can't be too careful, and there's been a lot of drama around Dumitru lately."

"That was *you* on the motorcycle?" Ree asked.

"I'm afraid so, and I called the guys to eliminate the threat. If I'd known you were friends of Axel's, I wouldn't have tried to get rid of you," Lizanne said. She carefully scanned outside the front window into the parking lot before disappearing into the back.

Ree climbed on top of the counter with the cash register and started pushing up the white ceiling tiles. Dust floated down like snow. She waved her hand in front of her face and turned away. She sneezed.

Quint grabbed the stool behind the counter and got to work on the computer.

"Found something," Ree said when he was still on his third attempt to get into the computer system. She pulled out a boot box. "This must be it."

He hurried over to her and grabbed her around the waist to help her down. She eased to sitting on the counter and set the boot box beside her, wiping the dust off.

"Wow, Axel wasn't kidding," she said after opening the box.

Quint released the breath he'd been holding. There were flash drives and Ziploc bags with what they could only assume was evidence inside them. "Everything he promised seems to be here."

"He was thorough," Ree stated. "All we have to do is verify the contents, and we should be able to get approval to make the arrest before the night is over."

"Ready to head back to the apartment?" he asked.

"As ready as I'll ever be," she said, and he realized exactly what that statement covered.

"Once we get the arrest warrant, we have another hill to climb," Quint stated as Lizanne emerged from the backroom.

"I know where Dumitru will be tonight," she said. She seemed as eager as they were to get Dumitru off the streets.

"Where is that?" Quint asked.

"The Dallas World Aquarium," she supplied. "It's a private party meant to reassure his people that everything is okay, and that's going to be the venue."

"It's a bold move," Quint said.

"He is in damage-control mode, showing his people that he is still in charge and can get one over on us," she explained.

"Makes sense in his twisted world." Quint realized she was holding something in her hand, a folded piece of paper. No, an invitation.

"This should get you through the door," she stated, handing it over. "I'd appreciate if you would leave my name out of it."

"No need to drag you into the middle of our fight," Quint reassured her.

"He's slippery, so he'll have a couple of exit plans," Lizanne said.

"Good to know," Quint said.

"Make sure you cover all the exits," she said. "And he'll always have an escape vehicle nearby. His favorite is a motorcycle. If you see one within a block of the place, it most likely belongs to him. But you can tell for certain if it has an all-seeing eye sticker on the helmet strapped to the back."

"Thank you for the information," Quint said.

"Just do us all a favor," she said, and she sounded exhausted. "Lock the sonofabitch up and throw away the key. We'll be better off."

"That's the plan," Quint stated.

"Before you head out," Lizanne started, twisting her fingers together. "Will Axel be okay?"

"He's in good hands," Quint promised.

"Thanks," she said.

Then she unceremoniously walked over to the door and unlocked it before heading to the backroom.

"We got what we needed," Quint said to Ree as they made their way back to the Jeep, arms full.

"All we need now is to secure the evidence and get the warrant," she said.

"We need to update Grappell as soon as we get out of this parking lot," he said. "I have a feeling hanging around here isn't good for our longevity."

Ree made eyes at him. Neither said another word until they were on the expressway again.

"I'll make the call," Ree said.

Grappell's voice came on the line after the second ring.

"What's happening?" he asked, and there was more than a hint of worry in his voice.

"We have everything we need to lock Dumitru up for the rest of his life if all the evidence checks out," Quint stated. "And we have a location. If we can get an arrest warrant in the next hour, I know where he'll be."

"On it," Grappell said. "Where are you now?"

"Heading back to the apartment, loaded with evidence," Quint stated.

"I'll have someone meet you in the parking garage," Grappell said. "Wait there."

The line went dead, but they both knew he would text or call back with the information about which agent and what kind of vehicle would meet them.

There was only one problem with the plan. The pregnancy test results waited upstairs, and they were both eager to check the stick.

"We go upstairs together," he said, hoping she agreed. This was their future, and they needed to face it together. Period. He wanted to be there for her no matter what the result turned out to be.

"Together." Ree liked the sound of that word. When he put it like that, she wasn't nearly as scared of the results. As long as they dealt with the news together, she could face this.

The text from Grappell came when they were halfway home. A banana-yellow Camaro would be arriving close to the same time as them. The driver would park behind them in the garage and be ready to flash his badge.

They were home within eight minutes of receiving the text, and the Camaro pulled in right behind them, as promised. Thankfully, there was no waiting around. They handed over the evidence, and then all they had to do was wait for the green light to raid the aquarium.

Oh, and one more thing, find out if they were going to be parents.

"Are you ready for this?" Quint asked, linking their fingers.

"As ready as I'll ever be," she confirmed. Her heart rate increased with every step toward the apartment. The elevator ride took her stomach away, and she could literally hear her heart racing in her ears as she walked the few steps to the front door.

Quint put the key in to unlock the door, and she noticed a slight tremble to his hand. Was he just as nervous as she was?

Quint held the door open a solid thirty seconds before Ree had the courage to walk through. She took in a deep breath and glanced down at her stomach. There was no way she was ready right now. Didn't mean she would never be or that she wouldn't pull it together if the answer came back pregnant.

Quint linked their fingers as they walked to the counter. One line. Not pregnant.

"Wow. That's good," Ree said as a whole host of

emotions washed over her and through her. Relief flooded her. "We're not ready for a—"

She glanced over at Quint, and his expression stopped her from continuing. There was a haunted look in his eyes, and she wondered if he was thinking about Tessa and the baby his friend lost.

"I'm sorry, Quint," she said, tugging him over.

He took the cue and brought her into an embrace.

"I thought you would be happy about the result," she whispered. "I'm confused."

"So am I," he stated. "I *should* be happy. I didn't think I wanted kids at all. Especially now, when it wasn't planned."

"Is it Tessa?" she asked. "Does this remind you of her and what she went through?"

"No," he said. "I can honestly say that I'm ready to move on and marry you. And, much to my own surprise, I'm ready to start a family whenever you are."

"It'll happen when the timing is right," she reassured him.

"All I have to do now is put the bastard behind bars who is responsible for Tessa's death," he said, clenching his back teeth as he finished his sentence.

And what if that didn't happen tonight? Would it ever be over? Would they ever be able to move on with their lives if the bust fell apart?

Chapter Twenty-Two

The map of the Dallas World Aquarium on Griffin Street in downtown Dallas had been studied. The blocks surrounding the place had been memorized. The plan to get in and get Dumitru was set. Best laid plans. Quint, of all people, knew how quickly everything could turn on a dime.

Having an idea of how they wanted this to go down helped with the nerves.

"Just the two of us are going in," Quint said, reviewing their notes while noticing how beautiful his future wife looked in a shimmering green minidress that brought out the emerald of her eyes. They were both dressed, wired and ready to go.

"But a team of five will be waiting on the outside. We'll have a pair of agents in a minivan parked across the street, Tex and Stanley. We'll have a jogger circling the area, Ben. And we'll have a couple strolling, Lisa and Evan. Tex and Stanley will be in full gear, ready and waiting. There'll be no mistaking them," Ree said. "We've both worked with the others or at the very least crossed paths with them."

"I could pick all our agents out of a lineup," he said, studying their photos in the database. They were pictured in several disguises to make it easier to spot them.

Quint kept his nose in the file as long as possible, doing his best to block out all the surprising feelings about the non-pregnancy. He should have been happy about the test result. After losing Tessa, had he blocked out any possibility of kids in his life? He still wondered if he'd be father material. And yet Ree's confidence in him had opened his heart to the possibility of a family.

Strange how losing something he never had in the first place caused an ache in his chest the size of Palo Duro Canyon. Life was confusing and strange. One thing was certain. He wanted to spend the rest of his life with Ree. It was the only thing he was one hundred percent sure about.

"I'll have my weapon, and you'll have yours," she said. "Once we spot Dumitru, we'll close in."

"No one will be too shocked about the two of us being there since we're known quantities," he said, circling back to the case.

"Once we get him in our sights, we'll make the call to the others for the raid," she said. "The other agents will grab as many folks as they can."

"We'll take down Dumitru," he said.

"Which should be easy since we'll already be standing within five feet of him," she said.

"Easy in theory," was all Quint said in response.

Ree's face said she agreed. "Let's go over the layout of the aquarium one more time."

"We should eat too," he said. "Who knows when we'll get the chance once this starts rolling?"

"Good point," she said. "I'm feeling a whole lot better. Should we order in?"

"I can probably pull together a meal based on leftovers," he said. "It'll be faster and will give me something to do."

"Waiting is the worst part," she said. He couldn't agree more.

Ten minutes later, they had a feast of two tacos, half a pizza and a salad. When this case was over, he was going to take a week off. The first couple of days, all he wanted to do was order in, be with Ree and sleep. He didn't care if they went to her place or his. On second thought, her mattress was far more comfortable than his. *Hers.*

It was good to make plans for what he intended to do after a bust. It was part of the process of envisioning how he wanted it to go down. It was a ritual he and Tessa had skipped that fateful day.

As he sat down to eat with Ree, he asked, "What's the first thing you're going to do when this is all over?"

"Kiss my fiancé before we start planning our honeymoon," she said with a smile that caused his chest to squeeze.

"I like the sound of that," he said, returning the smile and knowing it fell short of hers. "Our next mission will be our honeymoon. Count me in."

Ree practically beamed.

"I'd like to make peace with my mom too," she said after a thoughtful pause.

"That's another great idea," he stated. "There isn't a day that goes by I don't wish my mom was still here. Especially now. She would have loved you."

"I would have liked to spend time with her too," Ree said. "If we have a girl someday, I'd like to honor your mother by giving our daughter her name."

The sentence would have had the old Quint bolting out of the room to get fresh air. Now?

"I can't think of a better way to acknowledge her memory," he said. Kids? Who knew he'd be all in so fast after thinking he would never be fit for the responsibility?

That was the power of love, he thought.

"If we wrap this up tonight, we can make Sunday supper tomorrow," he pointed out.

"We could," she said. Again, the warmth in her smile could defrost a freezer in a matter of minutes.

"It's a date," he said. Ree reconciling with her mother would be huge. There was no reason to wait, either. It would only give her a chance to talk herself out of the decision. But the time had come for forward motion. No more being stuck in the past or letting the present dictate the future. The time had come for healing.

Quint's cell buzzed as they cleared the dishes. He checked the screen.

"It's go time," he said to Ree.

For what felt like a long moment, she stood there.

Then came, "We're ready for this. Let's finish what we started."

An ominous feeling settled over Quint. Past mistakes tried to edge their way in and break down his confidence. He shoved them aside and secured his weapon inside his ankle holster. Time to saddle up for the ride.

The first thing he noticed was the Jeep's flat tire, driver's side. Quint muttered a curse and prayed it wasn't a sign.

"I can help with that," Ree said, moving to the back of the vehicle where the spare was kept. Her high heels brought out the muscles in her calves.

"Normally, I'd be all for it, but you probably shouldn't get dirt all over you in that dress," he said. "You look incredible, by the way."

"Thanks," she said with another one of those smiles. "So do you."

"I'm wearing all black," he said with a laugh. "But, hey, I'll take the compliment."

He made the change in what had to be record time, and they were back on track within minutes. Ree sat in the passenger seat, not sulking exactly, but he could tell she wasn't thrilled with not being able to pitch in.

"Sorry," she mumbled, arms crossed.

"No worries," he reassured her. "You're already being tortured enough in those things strapped to your feet."

"That's true," she said with a half smile.

"Believe me when I say they look amazing on

you, but no one should have to wear stilts to walk around in," he said as he cranked the engine. The Check Engine light came on. "You have to be kidding me, right?"

"What is it?" she asked, probably distracted from the torture devices on her feet and her inability to throw her hair in a ponytail, roll up her sleeves and get a job done.

He pointed to the irritation.

"Ignore it," she said. "The dealer probably just wants to make money off us somehow."

"True. That light used to mean something," he agreed as he headed toward the aquarium.

"Yes, it meant pull your buns off the road as fast as you can and park this sucker until a tow truck arrives," she quipped.

"Not so much anymore," he stated.

"Funny how much has changed since my dad was alive. He taught me that long before I was old enough to drive," she said, and there was a hint of sadness to her tone. "I have a few vivid memories of him and not much else. I wish I'd known him better."

Quint reached over and covered her hand with his briefly. There were no words that could soothe the loss of a parent, so he didn't try. All he could do was sit there with her in her moment of sadness and not try to offer hollow words to make it better.

"Looks like we're there already," she said, turning her face to the window and, he guessed, wiping away a stray tear.

She cleared her throat.

"I'll park in the adjacent lot like the others," he said, pulling in and finding an open spot. He memorized the number, opened the parking app, and paid.

"Looks like the party is in full swing," she said, glancing around at the near-full parking lot.

"It does," he said, noting how much easier it would be on them if there were only a few people here. A crowd could turn to chaos in a heartbeat. They could get lost in throngs of people.

"We can walk around the building to check for the motorcycle," Ree said after they'd parked and paid.

He nodded before reaching for her hand. Apparently she had the same idea. They ended up meeting in the middle. A quick smile and nod later, and they were making the rounds. The motorcycle was parked directly behind a dumpster at the back exit of the building. How convenient. And, yes, the sticker was on the helmet that was strapped to the seat.

Quint pulled out a blade and slashed both tires.

"That will slow him down," he said as they casually walked the rest of the building. All he could think was that someone should have put a security detail on the bike, but he was glad they hadn't.

The aquarium layout was a labyrinth. The journey started at the front door and then wound through the building, leading Ree and Quint through various rooms that had a distinct look and feel as well as a different type of habitat for exotic birds, mammals and fish.

As they walked through the maze that was the aquarium, he scanned the faces. From the looks of it, the entire place had been rented. Ree was beside him, doing the same thing. The sound of a waterfall filled the air. Between that and the low hum of conversation, it would be impossible to pick out a particular voice. They were shoulder to shoulder as they looked for Dumitru.

Ree squeezed Quint's hand the moment she got confirmation everyone was in place. The cavalry had arrived. All was ready to go. Now all they needed was to find Dumitru. Quint searched face after face, looking for blond-haired, blue-eyed bastard. The man seemed more ghost than real at this point to Quint. Many had seen him from his inner circle. No one outside of it. He had a knack for disappearing at critical moments. Was he even here?

Waiters moved through the crowd with trays hoisted above the fray. They somehow managed to serve drinks.

At some point during the walk through the rain forest, Quint was handed a drink as they made their way to the immersive shark tunnel. If Quint was a betting man, he'd put money on Dumitru being there. What was it about criminals and sharks? Both opportunists? Kindred spirits?

There were more people at the mouth of the tunnel than seemed like there was space to fit them. Quint's adrenaline spiked and the hairs on the back of his neck pricked as they neared the crowd. The tunnel itself was impressive.

From behind them, someone was pushing through the crowd. Quint turned in time to see Lindy coming straight at them. Quint instinctively stepped in between Lindy and Ree, using his body to block the man from coming at her.

Quint cursed underneath his breath. This wasn't the time for a confrontation. Lindy could blow the whole night if he spooked Dumitru. Quint dropped Ree's hand as a furious Lindy came right at them.

He shoved Quint back a step, causing his drink to go flying. Arresting this jerk was going to be a pleasure when this night was all said and done. There was enough evidence against Lindy to lock him up for a very long time. But he wasn't the one Quint was after tonight.

"What the hell?" Quint asked, shoving Lindy right back.

Afterward he stood there with this arms folded across his chest, just daring Lindy to make another move.

"Where is she?" Lindy demanded.

"I have no idea," Quint shot back. He held his hands high in the air and glanced around, making a show of not hiding anything. "Why don't you tell us?"

Lindy reared his hand back in a flash, but Quint saw the punch coming from a mile away. He caught Lindy's fist as the man tried to punch Quint in the face. Then he squeezed, putting enough pressure on Lindy to come close to cracking a bone.

"You want it to go down like this?" Quint asked. He didn't dare remove his gaze from Lindy, but he could feel the tension in the area ratchet up. Since there were no metal detectors in use at the doors,

Quint realized it was possible that most everyone in the room would be packing. The last thing he wanted was a bloodbath.

"What's going on over here?" an unfamiliar voice asked from the dark tunnel behind them.

"Nothing," Lindy said, seeming to backpedal a little too fast.

"What does that mean?" the voice continued. "I heard something. Explain to me what it is."

"It's fine, Dumitru," one of the others consoled him, and there was a nervous note to his voice.

Since Lindy backed off, Quint risked turning around to get a good look. The crowd had parted like Moses was about to cross the Red Sea. The man Quint had been hunting for months stood there in the center of the tunnel, arms folded, in a show of dominance as a large shark swam overhead. Dumitru looked to be in his early forties, older than Quint expected, although he wasn't certain why. It made sense. He had sun-worn skin and tattoos peeking out of his expensive, tailored, silk button-down shirt. Quint guessed the man's height to be around five feet ten inches, and he had tree trunks for arms.

Ree had disappeared into the crowd forming around Quint. The thought of her being alone in this group sent an icy chill racing down Quint's back. But this was not the same situation as with Tessa.

Had she given the signal to the others to descend on the building? An earpiece would be a dead giveaway, so neither had one, but they were wired. Quint glanced around. Where was Ree?

Chapter Twenty-Three

Chaos could be good. It also could be deadly.

Ree used the moment of chaos created by Lindy coming at Quint to circle the crowd and position herself behind Dumitru. There were several folks in her line of sight, blocking a straightforward view of the happenings. She'd taken advantage of the opportunity presented. All she waited for now was to make eye contact with Quint so she could give the signal. If she got close enough to Dumitru, she would go ahead make the call for the team to come inside for an arrest.

This seemed like a good time to slip out of those high heels in case she needed to run. Ree sat on the wall, blocking visitors from getting too close to the glass in the tunnel. She quickly slipped out of her shoes, brandishing one to use as a weapon should the need arise. The heel was essentially a spike.

The crowd around her was on edge. She could feel the tension rising. It wouldn't take much to stir up mob mentality. Since everyone was most likely armed, this situation could get out of hand real quick if they weren't careful.

Standing up, she pushed up to her tiptoes, trying to get a look at Quint. She saw him just in time to watch two guys jump him, one on each side. The men started dragging him toward her and where she figured they were about to teach him a lesson.

"Move," one of the men said as Quint struggled, trying to break their grip.

Was he waiting for her?

"You never answered my question," Lindy said to Quint. He was one of the few people in the room who could identify Ree. She let her loose curls fall around her face, trying to use her hair as a shield.

Anger welled up inside her at the sight of him, standing there sneering as Quint was dragged past her.

"Take him to my office," Dumitru said, turning to follow Quint.

It was then that Quint glanced over at her and gave the slightest nod. She knew exactly what it meant. Go time.

Ree reached around behind her and pressed the button sewn into her dress's lining. The cavalry would arrive in a matter of minutes. She followed, being elbowed by the crowd as she made her way toward the back against the grain.

"Go back to the party," Dumitru announced, giving a quick wave of his hand.

Most stopped following, but there was no way she was letting Dumitru out of sight. In fact, she ended up a little too close to him because there was nowhere to go when he stopped and turned around. She nearly bumped right into him. Her clutch had a secret compartment that contained her badge and a pair of zip cuffs.

They belonged on Dumitru's wrists.

"Hey there, beautiful," he said, snatching her by the arm. His fingers dug into her forearm as he yanked her toward him.

She lost her balance and ended up smacking against him.

"That hurts," she said, glancing down at his grip.

"Good," he practically sneered. "It'll only get better later."

A literal shiver rocked her at the thought of being forced to do anything with this man other than place him under arrest.

"I have a message for you," she said, leaning toward him.

"Oh, yeah?" he asked. A smile that was probably meant to look sexy but ended up creepy split his face. "Is it what you're going to let me do to you later?"

"How about what I'm going to do to you right now," she said through half-clenched teeth. In the background, she caught a glimpse of two faces coming right at them, Grappell and Bjorn. The desk agent was average height and build, not exactly someone who spent his days at the gym but not heavyset either. He had red hair and blue eyes, and she was thrilled to see him heading toward her. Their boss was a couple steps in front of Grappell. Bjorn had on navy slacks and a white blouse. Blond hair with brown eyes, she was tall, fit, and could best be described as fierce.

"Good." Dumitru brought his hand up around the base of her neck and forced her face within an inch of his. "Because I can hardly wait to get started."

"I should start by telling you that you're under arrest," Ree stated.

The shocked look on Dumitru's face was priceless as she continued reading his Miranda rights.

His shock didn't last long. In fact, he threw an elbow into Ree's rib cage and tried to break free from the grip she now had on his wrist.

In the next couple of moments, Quint twisted free from the men holding him, and all hell broke loose as Bjorn and Grappell arrived on the scene.

Quint came at Dumitru like a linebacker going in for a sack. He ran him up against the wall, causing Dumitru to trip backwards. Ree drew her weapon and pointed it toward the gathering crowd as Ben bolted in.

"Hands where I can see them," Bjorn said to the group to no avail.

A voice came through loud and clear from a megaphone outside, though.

"You're surrounded by law enforcement. The best thing each of you can do is cooperate," the voice she recognized as belonging to Tex said.

The crowd scattered, but Quint was all over Dumitru. The next time he was standing upright, he was in cuffs, and his face was pressed against the wall.

"Where is Giselle?" Quint asked Dumitru. It took a couple of threats, but Dumitru finally said she was in the office. Stanley came out with her a few minutes later. Her eyes were red-rimmed and her face anguished.

"I didn't want anything to do with this," she said. "He threatened my boy and Axel isn't here to protect us. I'm so sorry for everything."

Ree wasn't a mother but she could imagine how powerful the need to protect a kid might be. After all, she'd watched her own mother try to keep Ree out of any possible danger.

Lisa and Evan rounded up as many folks as they could until the walls were literally lined with people, hands up.

The first thing Ree did when Dumitru was safely being led away was kiss her future husband. Then she excused herself and walked outside to get some fresh air.

Ree pulled out her cell phone and punched in her mother's number. The number would come through as unidentified, so she wasn't sure if her mom would answer. What she had to say couldn't wait.

Thankfully, her mother answered on the second ring.

"Mom, it's me, Ree," she started.

"Oh, Ree. I didn't recognize the number," her mother said, sounding concerned.

"I have a second phone for work and what I have to say to you couldn't wait," Ree continued. She needed to keep talking before she lost her nerve. "Mom, before you say anything else, I just want to tell you that I'm sorry I turned out to be a disappointment to you."

"What?" Her mother sounded confused now. "You're not a disappointment."

"It's okay, Mom. I know that I am. I don't bake things from scratch, and I'm sorry I never wore bows in my hair. How hard would it have been for me to let you put a bow in my hair?" she said.

"I'm the one who is sorry, Ree," her mother said. "You've always been strong-willed, and true, you were never the kind of girl who would let me dress you up in bows, but that doesn't mean you're a disappointment. I'm the one who should be sorry if that's how I've made you feel, because you gave me an even greater gift."

"I did?" Ree was the one confused now.

"That's right. I never had to worry about anyone taking advantage of you," her mother said. "You knew your own mind and how to stand up for yourself. That's far more useful than being able to bake a pie."

"But you love pie," Ree countered, still trying to process what her mother had just said.

"I love my stubborn daughter more," her mother said. "And I'm certain you came by your stubbornness honestly."

"Dad?" Ree asked.

"Oh, he could be stubborn when he wanted to be," her mother said. "But it's the women in the family who hold the record."

Ree laughed at that.

"I love you, Mom," she said.

"I love you too," her mother said. "And I wouldn't have had you any other way."

Tears streamed down Ree's cheeks as she turned back toward the building.

"Can you set a place at Sunday supper for me and my fiancé?" Ree asked.

"I'd love to," her mother said. She didn't ask who the man in Ree's life was. She had to know it was Quint, though.

"Then, we'll see you tomorrow," Ree said before ending the call. As she did, Quint came out the back door, his gaze searching for her.

"Over here," she said to her man, her future, her version of home.

He made a beeline toward her and immediately brought her into an embrace. There she stood for a long moment in the arms of the only man she could ever love.

"He's going away for a very long time," Quint said while he held her as though he hung on for dear life.

"Yes, he is," she agreed.

"Bjorn said Vadik will get visitation with his mother, who will stay in the facility where she is being well cared for," he continued.

"Good. That seems fair," she said before adding, "justice will be served with Dumitru. He didn't get away with it. Tessa didn't die in vain."

"No, she didn't," he said. "I will never forget her or her child."

"Good. Because I want you to tell me your stories. Tessa was a big part of your life. She was your best friend long before I met you. I want to hear all about your friendship and why it was special," she said to him.

"Okay," he said with a warmth that wrapped around her, soothed her. "Someday. I'll tell you all about our friendship. Right now, I'm ready to put the past behind me and think about the future. Dumitru will spend the rest of his life behind bars but that won't bring back Tessa or the baby. I've come to realize that obsessing over past mistakes won't make them any easier to get over."

"All that is true and I agree. But I want to get to know Tessa better. I hope that part of your past can move ahead with us," she said.

Quint brushed the backs of his fingers against her cheek.

"I've never met anyone like you, Ree," he said, catching her gaze and holding onto it. "And I could live a hundred years without finding another person who could hold a candle to you. I'm ready to put the past behind us, and step into our future. Together. I only want to take the good memories of Tessa with me from here on out."

"I think that's a wonderful plan," Ree said as she gazed into his eyes. Quint Casey. Her man. Her love. Her home.

Quint dipped his head down and kissed her, leaving no room for doubt they belonged together. And now, it was time to look to tomorrow instead of wishing the past could be different. It was time to embrace the life that lay ahead of them. Together forever.

Epilogue

Ree checked her reflection in the mirror one last time. She took in a deep breath as she stared at herself.

"Ready?" her mother asked, beaming with what looked a whole lot like pride.

"To marry Quint? Yes," Ree said, thinking she'd never seen a more beautiful dress than the one her mother had helped her pick out. "And thank you."

"For what?" mother asked.

"Everything," Ree said. "But mostly accepting me for who I am and being here to support me on this day."

"That was easy once I pushed aside my own stubbornness," her mother said with a sly smile and a wink. She really was the greatest person and Ree's older brother Shane had been right about Ree needing to lighten up when it came to their mother. But she had no intention of telling him that. There was no reason to give him a big head. "You really are beautiful. And I don't just mean in the dress."

"Love you, Mom," Ree said. "P.S., you're not supposed to make the bride cry on her wedding day. You'll ruin my makeup."

Her mother's warm smile brightened the moment.

A knock sounded at the door before her brother stuck his head inside.

"The reverend is here," he said, his gaze moving from their mother to Ree. "Wow. Sis. You look…"

He seemed to choke up on the last words. She couldn't have him getting too sentimental this early in the day.

"Like someone who could use a drink," she said with a smile.

"Nervous?" Shane asked, stepping inside and leaving the door open.

"Surprisingly, no," she said. She wasn't. Marrying Quint was the best thing she could imagine doing. "But I am ready."

Mother smiled before wiping a stray tear.

"Your grandfather is going to lose it when he sees how beautiful you look," Mother said, covering her own emotions with a cough. She took in a deep breath before placing her hands on Ree's shoulders. "This day will go by in a blur. Make sure to pay attention to the little moments and spend a few minutes with each person who cared enough to show up for you."

"I will," Ree said before embracing her mother one last time before walking down the aisle.

"The music is starting, Mom," Shane said. "You should go so you can be seated."

"Okay," Mother said before adding, "I love you both so much."

After another round of hugs, Shane held out his arm toward Ree.

"I refuse to give you away," he whispered as they exited the bride's room. "But I'm happy to bring Quint into the family."

Her brother's words had a calming effect on Ree.

"Thank you," she said to him. "For being the best big brother a person could ask for."

"Back at you, sis," he said as he walked her to the sanctuary of the church.

Everyone stood as they entered the room. Bjorn and Grappell were there, smiling from ear to ear. The aisle wasn't too long. Zoe, her maid of honor stood to the left. Angie stood next to Zoe. These two women were a critical part of Ree and Quint's love story. It only seemed right to include them in the ceremony.

To the right, Quint stood there with his hands clasped looking sexier than any groom had a right to. Next to him stood his best man and the person responsible for helping Quint become the human being he was today. Jazzy's look of pride nearly caused Ree's heart to burst. Jazzy held a puppy in his arms that seemed determined to wiggle out.

She looked at Quint, confused.

All he did was smile and nod in response, which confused her even more. Quint's best man had a little explaining to do, but she'd learned to expect pretty much anything when it came to her and Quint. Their relationship had its own pulse and she was learning to roll with it.

"Take good care of each other," was all Shane said as he joined Ree and Quint's hands.

After, Shane gave his sister a peck on the cheek before taking a seat with the family.

"The puppy is a wedding gift for you, by the way," Quint leaned forward and whispered. "I want you to have everything your heart desires and then some."

"I do," she said.

"The reverend hasn't asked us any questions yet," he said with a warm smile.

"Doesn't matter," she said. "I already do."

"Then I do too," he said.

There was a short ceremony that was immediately followed by a bone melting kiss. When Ree turned around, she skimmed the faces of those she loved and all the people who were important in their lives.

There was so much love and happiness in one room. She was ready to get started on forever. But first...cake.

* * * * *

In case you missed the previous books in
USA TODAY *bestselling author Barb Han's series,*
A Ree and Quint Novel, look for

Undercover Couple
Newlywed Assignment
Eyewitness Man and Wife

You'll find them wherever
Harlequin Intrigue books are sold!